SEX *meets* LIFE

SEX *meets* LIFE

Edited by Anna Sansom

Foreword by Meg-John Barker

Cover design by Anna Sansom & Esther Lemmens

Inner design & typesetting by Esther Lemmens
estherlemmens.com

Visit the editor's website at **AnnaSansom.com**

Disclaimer

This book is a collection of personal essays and short fiction. The views and experiences expressed within these works are those of the individual authors and do not necessarily reflect the views or opinions of the editor or the publisher.

Please be aware that some of the content in this book contains explicit descriptions of sexual acts, which may not be suitable for all readers. We encourage anyone engaging with this material to approach it with care and self-awareness, keeping in mind your own personal sensitivities and boundaries. Content themes are provided to help guide your decisions but these are not definitive.

This book is intended for adult readers only. The content is provided for literary and creative purposes, and should not be considered professional advice on relationships, sexual health, or personal well-being. The editor, authors, and publisher do not offer any guarantees regarding the accuracy, completeness, or applicability of the content for any particular purpose.

By reading this book, you acknowledge that the editor, authors, and publisher are not liable for any emotional distress, discomfort, or harm that may arise from engaging with the material. Furthermore, the editor, authors, and publisher are not responsible for how the content may be interpreted or applied by readers in their personal lives. Any decisions or actions taken based on the content of this book are the sole responsibility of the reader.

If any of the topics discussed raise concerns for you, or if you find the material emotionally challenging, we encourage you to seek appropriate support from a qualified professional.

By continuing to read this book, you agree to these terms and accept this disclaimer.

Acknowledgements

I extend my deepest gratitude to all the courageous authors who have shared their stories in this anthology. Thank you for being part of this co-creation and sharing my vision of a book that celebrates diversity and offers a platform for voices and stories that may not otherwise be heard. Thank you for trusting me with your words. I know it can feel like a vulnerable place but, truly, your stories matter and it is a gift that you have chosen to share them in this way. I hope you feel proud to be part of this extraordinary collection.

Thank you to MJ for your words of support and for writing an outstanding Foreword. I love seeing the book through your eyes and I'm grateful for your insights and reflections.

Thank you, Esther! You have made the final stages of publication such a joy. I'm grateful for your brilliant eye for detail and design, your organisational skills, and our friendship. Thank you for everything you've done to help get this project over the finish line.

I've talked about this book a *lot* over the last year or so. To all my friends and loved ones who listened, and who continue to accept me as 'that friend' who talks about things that aren't always talked about in polite company... thank you. True intimacy is being seen and loved as our authentic selves.

My thanks go to the generous supporters who donated to help fund the publication of this book. Your belief and trust in me, the authors, and our words, mean the world to me. You have helped validate this whole experience for me and I am grateful for your donations and your kindness. What a magnificent bunch of people you are!

Here is a list of the supporters who agreed to be named in the book:

AJ Pilling
Alice Tew
Allyssa Carlton
Audrey Boss
Bastian Verdel
Cathy Hilton
Charlotte Hueso
DK Green
Eleanor Campbell-West
Fiona Taylor
Hayley Jayne Daniels
Kitty Appleby
Lisa Tara Jackson
Lucy
Lucy Kayne
Marie Louise Cochrane
Martin Ousley
Neil Brown
Nick Harleigh-Bell
Nicola Humber
Susan Warren
Tania Glyde
Tim Brown

Lastly, my deepest, heartfelt love and thanks go to Bunny. Thank you for your patience and understanding while I poured my time and energy into this book. Thank you for bringing me endless cups of tea, and for the cuddles and words of encouragement that accompanied them (and the occasional home-baked scone!). Thank you for sticking by me as we've navigated so many life changes and for building a life where sex and intimacy are always evolving. Thank you for taking a leap of faith with me and thank you for the adventure that is our life together.

Contents

Disclaimer.. v

Acknowledgements vii

Foreword *by Meg-John Barker*..........................xi

Introduction *by Anna Sansom* xxiii

Silver Linings *by Alyx Marsh*..............................1

Losing My Religion (to Find My Divinity)
  by Bear Phillips 11

Sensitive Single Seeks Sexy Soulmate
  by Jennifer Cockcroft 21

Lightening Up: Adventures in Self-liberation
  by Esther Lemmens 39

Entering the Bardo *by Kimaya Crolla-Younger*............. 51

Becoming Me: a Story of Four Women and
  Two Men *by Eve Ray* 71

Horny Old Woman *by Joy Moates* 89

This, too, is Intimacy *by Esther Wild*............................99

Talk About the Passion: Confessions of an
  Insatiable, Demisexual Slut *by Jules Purnell* 103

Don't You Want Me? *by Lily Jenkins* 113

The Camel's Saddle *by AC Asquith*.............................. 129

Sex is the Easy Part *by Trine Lehmann Hansen* 137

Unbreakable *by Merryn August*.................................. 147

Earth-animal *by Britt Foster* 155

Our Capacity for Passion: Seasons of Sensuality
  by Maria Cyndi... 159

Let the Joy In *by Kaan K* 175

Masturbation Saved My Life *by Anna Sansom* 189

About the Editor... 197

Authors... 199

Permissions Acknowledgements................................. 207

Foreword

BY MEG-JOHN BARKER

When I heard that Anna was putting together this collection, I was immediately drawn to it and had to find out more. Over the last five years, I've been through profound shifts in how I relate to life: to myself, to others, and to the world around me. The erotic wove through all of these changes. It was part of what pulled everything out from under me in the first place, necessitating such a time of upheaval. It was one of the key practices which helped me navigate through such a terrible, beautiful process. And it was something that shifted as a result of going through this – ongoing – period of transformation.

You could say that sex met life, and also that life met sex, and that life and sex learnt to dance together in familiar and unfamiliar ways through these most challenging of years.

In her introduction, Anna talks about being in the messy middle: the liminal times when we're not who we were, but also not who we are to become. In the following chapter, Alyx uses the metaphor of the caterpillar who has to completely dissolve in the chrysalis in order to reemerge as a moth or butterfly. For a while, there is no caterpillar and also no flying insect, just goo. Nothing can prepare you for quite how vulnerable and frightening it is to be living your goo life!

Life: What we're up against

I was drawn to this collection because I wanted to hear from others who might have been through – or be going through – something like this.

Reading through the book, and reflecting on my own experiences, I was struck by the different levels on which life can confront us, necessitating such periods of change and transformation. I often use four Es for this:

- **Embodied:** We all have unique bodyminds, and can be confronted by the ways these change over time (e.g. menopause, ageing, disability), and by uncovering things we didn't previously know about how they work (e.g. unmasking neurodivergence, realising the presence of a chronic condition, or discovering how our bodyminds have been shaped by developmental/intergenerational trauma).

- **Entangled:** We're all inevitably in relation with others and are deeply impacted by changes in the ways they relate to us (e.g. intimacy with a significant person beginning, ending or transforming; finding or losing supportive community; or others relating with us in traumatised/traumatising ways – attacking us, abandoning us, or trying to trap us in certain ways of relating with them).

- **Embedded:** We're embedded in a time, place, and dominant culture, which gives us a strong sense of what it means to be a successful self, including how we should do sex, gender, and relationships. Through our experiences and choices, we may find ourselves confronted by the ways in which we're drawn to this culture and align with it and/or the ways we refuse or resist it. These things may shift and change many times, as may the wider culture itself, and what it values.

- **Existential:** We're existential beings, which means that we face (and/or try to avoid) the realities of life (e.g. change, pain, and mortality) and we try to make some meaning out of our experiences, perhaps in the form of creativity, spirituality, and/or a set of values.

Like so many authors in this book, the last few years confronted me on all of these levels. At the embodied level, I aged, I went through peri/menopause, I continued gender transitioning, I unmasked my autism, and I navigated long-virus-related disability. At the entangled level, I was profoundly impacted by relationship beginnings and endings, losses and changes, by an important therapeutic relationship, and by recognising – and confronting – my own relational trauma and how it played out with the relational trauma of others. At the embedded level – like all of us – I was hugely impacted by the global pandemic, by lockdown, and by all the ongoing crises starkly exposed during this tumultuous time. At the existential level, I went through break-up, break-down, and break-through with old avoidance patterns, with cultural norms, with creative and erotic practices, and more.

Of course, all these 'E' levels are deeply interconnected, as COVID-19 demonstrated: in the huge disparities in how our bodyminds responded to the virus, in how lockdown impacted us differently depending on whether we faced it alone and/or with others, and in whose lives were and weren't valued in community and political responses over time. While only a few authors in this collection – Jules, Maria Cyndi and Lily – mention COVID by name, the massive impact of the global pandemic can be felt through many chapters. Similarly, whether we experience menopause, realising our neurodivergence, or ageing as a triumph and/or tragedy, as something to be celebrated and/or commiserated with, depends hugely on the stories circulating about those things in wider culture, the systems and structures of support available or unavailable to us, and the reactions of the close people – and other beings – around us.

It was heartening to see my experiences reflected through the chapters of this book, and I was also struck by the diversity of ways in which such experiences can impact us – separately and in combination – depending on who we are, what else we've been through, and how we engage with them.

Sex: Challenging cultures of 'normal'

In order to embrace the shifts and changes that life brought their way, the contributors to this collection had to question the dominant culture's norms and ideals around sex in various ways, challenging taken-for-granted assumptions about how bodies should look and work, how desire should be felt and expressed, and more. Here are a few examples.

Many of us learn – through education, media representations, and relationships – that our sexual 'orientation' will be fixed throughout our lives, and that it will be all about the gender of the people who we are attracted to. Echoing the findings of researchers like Lisa Diamond, the contributors to this book demonstrate that our sexual identities and experiences can and do change over time, as in Eve and Alyx's chapters where authors/characters become attracted to people of different genders than before. Contributors also support the theories of scholars like Sari Van Anders who emphasise that there's a lot more to sexuality than gender of attraction. Through the chapters we read about people discovering, or shifting into, various ace-spectrum sexualities (demisexuality, asexuality, grey-A), as well as moving towards – or away from – various forms of kink and non-monogamy, solo sex and partnered sex, and sex within different kinds of emotional and/or erotic, personal and/or professional, relationships.

Mainstream sex therapy and research often suggest that people should remain sexual in a certain specific way over time, and that people in 'successful' relationships should keep having sex of the same type and frequency. If not, there is a problem. These ideas are so entrenched that – according to the UK national survey of sexual attitudes and lifestyles – around a half of people see themselves as having some kind of sexual 'dysfunction'. Authors in this collection model the reality that our levels of desire, and sex in relationships, fluctuate hugely over time. Britt and Jennifer step into and out of periods of intentional celibacy; Alyx, Esther L., Esther W., Maria Cyndi, and Lily's character Louise navigate shifts in the amount of sex in their relationships in diverse ways. Anna, Bear, Jules, Trine, AC, and Kaan's character Red explore different kinds of sex and intimacy – with themselves and others – than they've experienced before, while Joy, Merryn and Kimaya find new ways to keep important aspects of their sexualities alive in the face of huge life changes.

Mainstream culture defines only certain bodies as sexually attractive, desirable, or functional, suggesting that we should try to hold onto such bodies for as long as possible, and that those who fall far from the ideal simply shouldn't attempt to be sexual or intimate with others. Authors in this collection offer some vital challenges to the common notions that ageing bodies are less desirable or desiring (Joy), that menopause necessarily means feeling less desire (Alyx, Maria Cyndi, Lily's character Louise), that disabled people are not sexual (Maria Cyndi, Kimaya), and that it's impossible to imagine erotic intimacy in the context of chronic pain and illness (Jennifer, Merryn).

Finally, Trine, Eve, Anna and Britt all offer important challenges to the assumption that the most important relationships in our lives are necessarily sexual ones, with celebrations of the ways in which friendships can affirm our sexualities, and explorations of non-sexual forms of intimacy.

Creating supportive alternative cultures

Throughout my own work on sex over the years it's always felt important to reveal the damage that limiting cultural norms and ideals about sex do, and to share the wisdom from people who are marginalised in their sexualities about what sex can be like, if we approach it with openness, curiosity, consciousness and care. This book resonates strongly with that project as it demonstrates what might be possible if we could learn to embrace uncertainty and stay present with all our feelings about our ever-changing, complex, multifaceted sexualities.

Such things are hard – if not impossible – if the culture and people around us constantly present one rigid, limited, kind of sex as the only acceptable possibility, and suggest that anything else is some kind of deviance or failing. Trailblazing books like this create vital alternative subcultures and possibility models that we can turn to during the long, slow process of wider cultural transformation.

For those of us going through periods of challenge and change, a collection like this offers many important supports:

- It normalises such times, showing us that we are not alone in these experiences, nor in finding them painful, terrifying, enraging, shameful, and every other feeling that courses through us, often all at once.
- It gives us a sense of connection with others, and solidarity in the kind of courage that's required when we surrender and/or commit to such change, particularly given how much this requires challenging long-held survival strategies and/or entrenched cultural norms.
- It provides a thread of hope – like the string through the labyrinth – even if that string stretches impossibly thin at times. If others have made it through something like this and eventually been glad that they did, perhaps I can do it too.
- It presents us with suggestions of practices and processes, resources and rituals, that might help us to meet these challenges.
- It demonstrates, over and over, the value of embracing the uncertainty of life, even as we inevitably attempt to find something we can control, something to hold onto, some stable sense of self, or sex, or anything!

Alert to the importance of moving beyond binaries as I am, I'm struck by the many binaries the chapters in this collection take us beyond, in addition to celebrating the sticky, messy in-between space of goo life. Have some more dot points!

- As Anna says, these kinds of stories move us beyond the cultural binary of idealising our sex/uality or seeing it as a problem to be fixed.

- They invite us to question whether we are finding something and/or losing something, whether something is dying and/or being (re)born, alerting us to the potential of the both/and, and the cyclical nature of things.
- They demonstrate how connected we are by the challenges of life and how we respond to them, as well as what a vast diversity of experiences we can go through, and how differently they can impact us. I'm thinking, for example, of the similar and different experiences of peri/menopause described by Anna, Alyx, Maria Cyndi, Esther L., and Louise (in Lily's chapter).
- They show how the changes we go through can be consciously pursued, as in Bear's account of stepping into his power or Eve and Kaan's descriptions of gender transition. And how they can be thrust upon us by circumstances, others, or wider culture, as in Merryn's experience of bereavement or Kimaya's of requiring care. And how it's often a complex combination of the two.
- They highlight how, chosen and/or imposed, they can both open up and close down our possibilities, expanding and contracting our erotic – and other – capacities, often in surprising, unexpected ways.

Meeting the challenge

I hope that readers of this book will come away with clarity that there is no 'one size fits all' way of facing these kinds of challenges. In addition to feeling and responding differently to shifts in desire, menopause, or transition, for example, different approaches to such things also work for different people, and at different times in their lives.

It's important to be cautious around any 'expert', community, or close person who gives the impression that they know the path you need to follow better than you know it yourself. Even when we're at our most deeply confused and desperate – and these times certainly often take us to such places – it's vital that we find our own ways through, ideally with a lot of support from others, but never with them taking over and disempowering us by imposing their understandings or approaches. AC Asquith's chapter, in particular, beautifully demonstrates the ways in which we might reframe the 'expertise' we've learnt about sex from our culture, faith, or community through our own explorations.

The diverse ways in which people met the challenges they were faced with struck me again and again as I read through this book. For example, some of us turned inwards towards self-exploration and self-compassion. Others turned in the exact opposite direction towards intimacy or community. Some embraced the opportunities that are currently available – through dating technologies or cuddle clubs, for example. Others sought alternative paths or imagined futures beyond what is possible now. Some found creativity a useful outlet or place of exploration through times of change, others disconnected from previously valued forms of creativity. Perhaps we often have to swing from one end of the pendulum to the other when facing major changes, before finding a more steady place, or deciding to continue to swing.

For me, a key thread through this whole time has been embracing plurality. Explorations in erotic memoir and fiction led me to an increasing awareness that I contained many selves, not just one. Bringing these selves into erotic play with others enabled us (plurally) to understand that we went much further than being sexual roles or kink headspaces, and that we needed to come into deep relationship – with ourselves and others – beyond the erotic/ romantic. Alongside meditation, journaling and other tools, erotic fantasy and fiction were important steadying and explorative practices through our years of deep retreat and therapy, while we worked through the trauma many of us carried and the traumatised/traumatising relational patterns this had resulted in.

While few of the contributors to this collection mention plurality explicitly, we were heartened to find resonances here with authors who described experiences of: realising that they weren't who they'd previously thought they were; detaching from ways they'd been stuck in cultural norms or in the expectations of others; being surprised by fearful and raging energies suddenly coming through them; finding inner/outer wild, wise, compassionate or vulnerable aspects; and relating with past and/or possible future erotic selves.

Also, plurality of feeling is very present throughout the collection, as most chapters in some way emphasise the importance of feeling whatever we feel about what we're going through, being with the full range of emotions that life changes can bring up, and perhaps weaving our big, complex feelings explicitly into our solo or partnered sex practices, and/or into our work as erotic writers or sexual professionals. Bear, Anna, Merryn, Trine, Esther W. and Kimaya particularly explore this kind of territory, but many touch on it.

Compassion

The final thing I'd like to emphasise in this foreword is compassion. It's hard to really capture the enormity of what we're all up against at the moment. Multiple crises face the world, revealing just how vulnerable we are, and often resulting in ourselves, others, and whole communities reacting in painful ways in desperate attempts to get some ground (back) under our feet.

Marginalised people – as all those included in this book are in one way or another – bear the brunt of these traumatised and traumatising times, as we see in the global rise in misogynist and queerphobic political parties, the moral panics around trans, and the rolling back of anything like good sex and relationship education.

The sexual communities that I've been aligned with over the years – bi+, non-monogamous, kink, queer, conscious sex, and more – have seen far too many people fall off the edge in recent years, and far more of us get terribly close to that. In addition to these deaths, there have been painful rifts and ruptures which have reverberated through communities, leaving many fearfully retreating into isolation, and often severely limiting the capacities of those who remain to support one another.

My sense is that, with our deepening understandings of trauma, neurodivergence, consent, and more, we're just at the beginning of learning how we might respond to crises – in ourselves, in our relationships and communities, and in the world – in ways that don't just become part *of* the crisis, as Báyò Akómoláfé puts it.

It takes great courage for people to be as real and vulnerable at such times as the authors in this collection have been: speaking the truth of their lived experience even while knowing that they are messy (goo) in places, and that their words and actions are inevitably imperfect. This is even more the case when the themes being written about involve such tender territory as our erotic and intimate lives, our trauma and our pain.

I'd invite you to read this collection with as much compassion as you can muster for the authors and for yourselves. Perhaps we might find the *most* compassion for the places where we've been hurt, where we've acted out of our pain in ways that have hurt others, and where we struggle to *find* compassion. It's a long journey we're all on and wherever we've got to at this point is okay. It has to be.

Introduction

BY ANNA SANSOM

Have you heard the one about the erotic writer who lost her libido? Well, that was me – and it was no joke, I can tell you.

Yep, after over two decades of writing smut, and living out a variety of my fantasies in real life too, I found myself feeling… lost.

I wasn't just an erotic writer; I'd also written the Sex/Life column for DIVA Magazine for two years and interviewed all sorts of people about their sex lives. I'd run workshops and events for other people to explore their fantasies and desires – on the page as well as in the bedroom.

This was what I *did*. Now what was I going *to do?*

If I wasn't the person who thought about sex, who wrote about desire, love and lust, and who shared her thoughts and writings with other people, who was I?

On the surface, it probably looked like I was going through a midlife crisis. As I swopped my 40s for my 50s, and as perimenopause did her darndest to strip me of any certainty or familiarity in my body and emotions, my libido quietly retreated into the background.

This was problematic for many reasons: my identity, my passion, my purpose... all felt like they'd been the victims of an alien abduction. The 'me' I once knew and had learned how to love was now a million light years away.

And it wasn't just me who felt the loss: my partner of over 20 years had to adjust to this new, subdued version of my sexuality too.

Thankfully, without knowing it at the time, the younger me had created a time capsule of my desire. I'd written a book called *Desire Lines* and, in it, I'd clearly stated my life-long commitment to retaining my "desire for desire". No matter what life threw at me, I reasoned, as long as I had that commitment, and an understanding of my fundamental drives and needs when it came to sex and intimacy, I'd be okay. I'd always find my way back.

There was another truism in that book: my sexuality and my creativity are ultimately interconnected. Meaning, if I can't find the doorway into one, I can use the back door of the other to access the same space. Writing is my main creative outlet and so it is through the *act* of writing erotica that I can access my own eroticism.

I gave myself permission to write erotica from my current place – rather than feeling it had to be the same as it had been in the past. The result of this has been a whole new genre of erotica for me – my writing now encompasses more of the 'fantastic realities' of sexuality than pure fantasies. I've become more curious about how to create hot sex and deep intimacy when we allow imperfect moments, people, and outcomes. (Quite wonderfully, this evolution has led to my writing being selected for the crème de la crème of publication opportunities for erotica writers and a story of mine in Best Women's Erotica of the Year, Volume 10.)

Around the same time as I was facing up to my libido's unsanctioned space encounters, another significant event happened: a friend I'd known as part of an earth-based spiritual group I was a member of revealed to me her transphobia. As a proud member of the LGBTQIA+ community, who naively believed that my friends were allies (if not queer or trans themselves), I was shaken. My bubble popped abruptly and I felt raw, exposed, and deeply saddened.

I sought refuge in my creativity again, this time with a burning need to take some kind of *affirmative action*. I needed to do something to try and cancel out the negativity by adding something beautiful and inclusive to the world. I needed something that would be compassionate and *a celebration of diversity*.

My ideas, experiences, and curiosities converged and the idea for this book was birthed:

A book that would share stories of what happens to our sexual selves when life inevitably happens. A book that asks the question many of us would rather avoid: if we are no longer who we once were, but not yet who are to become, what happens to our sex lives in the messy middle? And by "we" I wanted to include a variety of voices of different backgrounds, different life experiences, and different desires. I wanted to show that 'different' doesn't mean unrelatable.

There are universal themes that run through all of our stories regardless of gender, sexual orientation, relationship status, age, or the way our bodies function:

The need to be loved and appreciated for who you truly are.
The desire to feel good in your body.
Wanting to share intimacy in ways that are personally meaningful and fulfilling.

I recently heard someone say that empathy is not about knowing what it's like to walk in another person's shoes. Rather, it's about believing the other person when they share *how they experience life in their shoes.*

Surely, we all want our lived experiences to be believed and validated? Yes, for many people sex and sexuality are deeply private aspects of their lives, but those who are brave enough (and feel safe enough) to authentically share this aspect of themselves more publicly, offer us a great gift.

Because, as we go through life, none of us know what's waiting around the corner. Change is inevitable. For some, health issues might be a factor. For others, we may find ourselves questioning who and what we are attracted to, and/or how we experience our gender. Relationships may form, evolve, or dissolve. All of us will age.

As part of my commitment to retaining my "desire for desire" I'd been curious about other people's experiences of navigating changes in their sex/lives – curious about what I could learn from them and also how their experiences could help to affirm that I wasn't the only person on this planet grappling with my identity and behaviours as a sexual person.

I reached out to some people I knew to ask if they would share their experiences in this book. I asked them to write about times of change: how they had or still were navigating these; and their reflections on the effects of these changes on their sexual identity, relationships, and desires. I also put out an open call for people to write about "finding, losing, and reimagining our sexual selves". I invited them to be raw and honest, to not hold anything back, and to share without the need to sanitise the truth of what it means to be messy and imperfect.

The resulting story collection contained in *Sex Meets Life* offers an alternative to mainstream messages which either idealise people's sex lives or view them as a problem to be fixed. The varied and diverse stories in this anthology will help you to see that the experience of finding your sex life in a state of flux or uncertainty is universal and that some form of change is inevitable. I hope that, after reading this collection, you will feel less isolated and more empowered to experience the kind/s of sex, intimacy, and pleasure you want and need as you go through life.

In *Sex Meets Life* you'll find stories from cis and trans women and men and non-binary folk, those who identify as straight, queer, demisexual, pansexual and more, those living with chronic illness and disability and others who don't, people in their 20s through to their 70s, and those in different relationship circumstances (solo, monogamous, poly and exploring).

In this unique collection from authors in the UK, USA, Europe, and Australia, you'll read about desire, passion, transformation, and evolution. Some of the stories include explicit details of sexual acts – including penetration, oral sex, masturbation, kink and BDSM. All of the stories contain honest and vulnerable accounts of what sex and intimacy mean to the author. We invite you to read with an open mind and heart. Take what is helpful for you and leave what is not.

You may see your own story reflected in these pieces. You may relate to the tales of imperfect intimacy and messy middles. You may gain new perspectives, comfort, or renewed passion.

Mostly, I hope you will feel part of this collective experience and understand that there are many intersections and opportunities to explore when *Sex Meets Life*.

The authors and their stories:

Alyx Marsh's (they/them) rising desire in menopause, and new confidence in their body, helped overcome a longstanding fear of intimacy and led to a confession to their husband of 30 years. The life changes that followed have been unexpected *'Silver Linings'*.

Bear Phillips (he/him) opens up about what it might mean to be a "safe man", how he can be in his power without stripping others of theirs, and how intimate presence can offer healing and wholeness. His journey of *'Losing My Religion (to Find My Divinity)'* is one from shame to sovereignty.

In *'Sensitive Single Seeks Sexy Soulmate'*, **Jennifer Cockcroft's** (she/her) life-inspired-fiction starts with a conversation with a healthcare professional and a decision to re-enter the world of dating after 15 years of celibacy, whilst living with a chronic illness. Will reality live up to the fantasy?

When her partner came out as asexual, **Esther Lemmens** (she/they) began to question her own past experiences and conditioning around sexuality. In *'Lightening Up'*, they describe their journey of self-liberation and all the new opportunities this offers.

In *'Entering the Bardo'*, **Kimaya Crolla-Younger** (she/her) shares how she faced the brutal pressure of her experience of suddenly becoming a wheelchair user in her 50s, by uncompromisingly opening her sensuous capacity to feel it all, and taking it all inside herself as 'compost for Eros'.

For **Eve Ray** (she/her), a later-in-life trans woman, the support and acceptance of her female friendship group was an essential part of her journey to *'Becoming Me'*. She offers us "Emma's" story, a semi-fictional and explicit account of discovery (of gender, bisexuality, and kink) and emergence.

Joy Moates (she/her) shares a call to arms for women who, like her, are over 70 and want to enthusiastically enjoy and celebrate their sexuality. In a society that insists she's too old to be sexual, she proudly claims the title of *'Horny Old Woman'*.

In *'This, too, is Intimacy'*, **Esther Wild** (she/her) shares what it's like to be a member of the 'sandwich generation' – simultaneously caring for children and ageing parents, whilst navigating her own health needs. By necessity, intimacy with her husband now looks very different to how it once was.

In *'Talk About the Passion: Confessions of an Insatiable, Demisexual Slut'*, **Jules Purnell** (they/he) explores how a need for passion *and* deep, emotional connection drives them, and what this means for a relationship with themself and others.

Lily Jenkins (she/her) introduces us to Louise: a woman who has entered midlife, whose children have left home, and whose career is going well. Her husband, however, won't have sex with her. *'Don't You Want Me?'* is a fictional account where Louise reunites with an old flame.

Having lived as a practising Muslim for most of her adult life, **AC Asquith (she/her)** is now exploring a new life with her non-binary partner. She offers an explicit account of this sexual awakening in *'The Camel's Saddle'*, and the myriad of ways this contrasts with her former life.

Trine Lehmann Hansen (she/her) has always felt that *'Sex is the Easy Part'*. Intimacy, however, is a whole different ballgame. An opportunity to join a Cuddle Club opens a doorway to intimacy for her – one that she knows won't lead to sex – and she shares the revelations and new opportunities this brings.

Merryn August (they/them), a queer person navigating bereavement and chronic pain, reframes what their kink identity means in the light of loss. Do they need to be *'Unbreakable'* to keep this essential part of themselves alive?

Britt Foster (she/they) recounts her attempts to determine the shape of her gender through the people she had sex with, and through intentional celibacy. Perhaps their gender is best described as *'Earth-animal'*.

In **'Our Capacity for Passion: Seasons of Sensuality'**, sex and disability activist, **Maria Cyndi**, shares how she reclaimed her body – and her pleasure – during the challenges of medical intervention, motherhood, and menopause. She reflects on the wisdom and ongoing commitment that accompany her and her husband into their next decade of desire.

Kaan K (they/them) shares a futuristic vision of trans sex and intimacy. This speculative fiction breaks the mould in many ways, and invites us to **'Let the Joy In'**.

Anna Sansom (she/her) is a wanker and proud. In **'Masturbation Saved My Life'** she recounts her unorthodox approach to self-pleasuring and what it gives her beyond simply being a way to get herself off.

SEX meets LIFE

Silver Linings

BY ALYX MARSH

Content: *perimenopause, deepening intimacy, sexual awakening,*
body changes, midlife evolution

I was never good at intimacy. It scared me, so I did what I could to avoid it. I was acting out of fear, which was mainly fear of rejection. Whenever I shared something personal, waiting for a reply was excruciating because I learned that my sharing would often be met with ridicule, judgement and derision. The rejection of my real, authentic self by another was intensely shaming. It was a sign that I was wrong somehow and wasn't good enough for others.

So, I learned to close myself down. I became almost incapable of connecting with another person on that deep level. I could feel them offering a connection, but I would reject it. I would deny that closeness in favour of safety – while craving it nonetheless.

Surface intimacy became my sanctuary. It was a safe place where I never went too deep and didn't offer my full self to another. I thought I had nailed this intimacy business because I could exist there without too much fear. But it became obvious it was a false protection where safety prevailed at the expense of growth.

Despite all that safety, the craving for connection became stronger, almost visceral. Life began to force me to see how and where I missed out. I saw how missed connections with others left nothing but gaping holes in my life, and overriding loneliness. I saw what others had, and I wanted that for myself.

With the denial and the refusal of intimacy came a lack of exploration and experimenting, which, of course, meant any sort of eroticism was pretty much a non-event. The lack of intimacy contributed to a dulling of my senses. It was too hard to change, to explore. Pain was involved with exploring and failing, but I didn't know I was allowed to fail. And I certainly didn't know I was allowed to get back up and keep going, keep exploring. Wanting more, becoming an explorer, and learning to experiment wasn't a slight on my character at all.

I had been taught to be grateful for what I had, and to want more was to be an ungrateful human, or worse, an ungrateful woman. How dare I aim above my station!

I want intimacy; I crave it with my whole self. I want all the things that go along with it. I want that deep connection; I want to be seen and loved and valued for who I am. For all the parts of me.

And that requires change.

Change is fucking hard; to begin is hard, and it's still hard when you're bogged down in the middle of it. Especially when it has been forced on you, even if it is ultimately for your own good. Everything feels awkward and wrong, yet at the same time, it feels right. As though this part of life was meant to happen, and here I am changing, evolving, and rebirthing myself.

I'm currently in the thick of perimenopause and doing my best to address and live with all the changes I'm going through. Most of these changes I have welcomed with open arms. I don't care what people think of me any more, of how I dress and look, what I do or don't do for a living, my hobbies and interests, my political persuasions, my beliefs and values... all that stuff. Many of my fucks have flown. At no other point in my life have I felt so content with who I am and who I am becoming.

Other changes, however, have caught me off guard. The physical changes of perimenopause were expected. I knew that menopause would eventually arrive, and I was gearing up to welcome it, but I wasn't ready for exactly how these changes would happen and how they would affect all of me. Mentally, physically, and emotionally, my whole system, my whole body, has been fundamentally changed. Irrevocably.

Some changes were disguised as losses. I gave up a job I enjoyed because of very heavy bleeding, and I'm still dealing with the fallout from that. I carry a lot more weight than I'd like and also have a lot less energy (cause and effect much?). Nor can I multitask any more (not that I want to). However, the silver lining to having limited energy is that I have become incredibly selective with what and who I spend my energy on. Only the most important things are being dealt with, and I'm not sorry.

I'm surprised by just how much my body has and is changing. Lack of muscle and tone, reduced flexibility, aches and pains that appear out of nowhere, tiredness that hits me like a brick wall and the necessity of daytime napping. Perhaps the greatest surprise has been the occasional yet disturbing sudden inability to reach orgasm – those times when it feels snatched away by some unseen force that seems to be intent on depriving me of one of my favourite forms of pleasure.

Of course, that development forced the realisation that now there is no outcome, there is no bullseye that must be hit for sex to be 'real'. Now it is a complete focus on pleasure for its own sake, and I'm okay with that.

Another unexpected silver lining to these changes is deepening intimacy with my partner. I'm not afraid to voice my frustrations and grief any more. I'm not afraid to tell it how it is. He asks with genuine interest how I'm feeling and what's happening to me that day. He sympathises with my frustrations, anger, and despair. He's the shoulder I cry on when nothing is going right. He's the one who tells me off when I fixate on some part of me not being 'right'; I am still the same person, and he thinks I am perfect.

Brain fog descended, which lasted for a few years in my case, but I certainly wasn't prepared for perimenopause to steal my words. I'm a writer. How can I call myself a writer if I can't find my words? I could always spell but even that ability has taken a hit.

I'm on an HRT journey now as I had an IUD inserted a few weeks ago, and I'm still dealing with the effects of that. Constant bleeding and occasional intense cramping seem to be my companions at the moment. I'm not happy about this situation, but there is a bright side. The brain fog has mostly lifted, and I am finding my words again. Not always, but it's a definite improvement. I felt like I had been taken over by someone or something else, and I just wasn't myself any more, so I'm glad to be back in what appears to be a new me.

In spite of the difficulties I'm going through, I like the new chapter that is being written for me, although sometimes it feels like a whole new book in a different genre. I have the very real sense of walking through a doorway, a portal, fully knowing I can't go back. And you know what? I really don't want to. That part of my life is over; I've lived it, and now I'm looking to the future.

I'm much more excited about what's in store for me. I know I can handle what comes my way. That doesn't mean that I won't get knocked over or that there won't be grief and sadness, but it does mean that I can work my way through those changes and come out better in the end.

Right now, I'm the caterpillar, my body nothing but goo, as I hunker down in my chrysalis, changing and evolving, waiting to be reborn into a butterfly. And I know my wings will be rainbow-coloured!

Coming out to my partner of over thirty years and admitting my feelings about women and non-binary people was hard. Lots of tears and fears about the future. But we have talked about it; he has had many thoughts, and we are at least having conversations about the future – about our future.

My desire for deeper intimacy led to me admitting my partner into my most private inner world, which has been eye-opening. I was frightened about his response to my confession, and his initial reaction was to be expected. But he returned to me a few days later with a more measured and thought-out response. My admission has opened a door that cannot be closed again.

This thing that I was so terrified of doing has proved to be one of the best things I have ever done. It has truly brought us together a lot more. We were drifting apart, partly due to my fears and reluctance to admit what was going on with me.

Still, we are looking to the future, planning the next

chapter of our relationship with added considerations and exploration.

I laugh at myself now with my desire to explore and experiment at fifty-two, considering how lousy I've been with intimacy and eroticism. The me in her twenties would never have considered doing this – I never liked my body. And the thought of doing this in my fifties certainly wasn't on my radar. So why now? I thought the wrinkles and sagging and extra weight would have me hiding away, believing my time to be up and my sex life over. Little did I know I would find an increased desire to uncover what exactly pleasure is and what that means for me. There is a hunger to know my body better, to map its pleasure zones and to find out what gives me deep, deep bliss.

My sexual desire is strong, perhaps stronger than it's ever been. Some would say that I'm lucky in that regard. I may just be one of those for whom perimenopause doesn't mean a decrease in desire. But I am still coy in stating my desires. I've been a habitual performer of desire smuggling, keeping the tightest lid on what I really want to feel and experience.

Now I've begun to ask for more. More of what I want and what I need to feel alive, nurtured, held, supported, and heard. And physical pleasure has been at the forefront of this. Opening myself up to my own desires and feeding them willingly. There is such a deep hunger to do that. I don't want to settle for anything less than I want, which brings its own issues and challenges. Things must be done differently, which means communication and negotiation.

My body sometimes feels like it has given up. The occasional inability to orgasm does distress me. I have that wonderful build-up, surfing all those delicious waves of pleasure, each one higher and stronger than the last. Only for it to disappear at the crest of the largest wave, evaporating into the ether. I'm left bewildered and floundering in the wash, struggling for an explanation. Why does this happen? I have no answers, but I take a small comfort in knowing it doesn't happen every time.

An orgasm was always the benchmark of 'great sex' – it's what I learned many years ago and kept holding on to – but now the goalposts have shifted. It's an adjustment, but it's not impossible. I don't feel bereft for not having an orgasm because, if I'm honest, sometimes I just don't have the energy for it. I know the benefits of orgasms for my body, but I'm not going to force it when I know that it's not going to happen.

I wasn't prepared for just how much I would change and evolve because of perimenopause. I am becoming a new person, of that I am certain. I will miss some aspects of me, but I look forward to who I am becoming. Each day reveals a tiny bit more of my journey.

These changes now feel like the seasons to me. That cyclical way of living, knowing that each season has its own time, rhythm, and reason. There is a purpose for the seasons just as there is a purpose for human changes and evolutions.

I'm an autumn person (which is my birthday), so going inwards – hibernating – doesn't faze me. I enjoy the shorter days, the crisp nights, and the slowing down into rest and rejuvenation. The knowledge of the cold and darkness to come has become an invitation to rest, reflect, and recuperate.

Wintertime, and my body is going to sleep. I have less energy to spend – I can't stand being 'busy' any more. Are my physical issues a way of my body telling me I need to rest? Wintering, which can be hard with its darkness and chill, is made easier by knowing that there will be a spring afterwards. There is sunlight, warmth, and new life when the wheel turns again. It is a hope I hold on to, given to me by those who have passed through their own life wintering before me.

I'm watching my horse shed her winter coat two weeks early this year. It takes time for her to moult fully, usually around a month or so. When moulting finishes, she comes into her first season of the year. At this time, I usually leave her alone for a month: her hormones run rampant, and it's best to stand to one side, offering food and treats with a well-outstretched hand, bowing with reverence as I leave my queen's yard, eternally grateful she has allowed me into her presence. But as she ages (she's 20 now), the force of her hormones has lessened somewhat. She still cycles, but it's not as evident as in past years. She is easier to deal with now, but she also knows the longer she hangs around me, the more food she'll get. She's me in horse form.

Surprisingly, I'm craving spring and summer this year. Where is the warmth? I need heat and sun, I want bare feet and less clothing. I want the warm summer sun reddening my skin and filling me with energy, excitement and aliveness. Summer means the beach and swimming, revelling in my skin and the way it feels being exposed to the elements. It's an erotic season, with bare skin on display, fewer clothes worn, and juicy summer fruit dripping with nectar. Languid days and even more languid nights. At least that's what I try to remind myself when the reality is more of a humid, sweaty nature, complete with lack of sleep from nights of stifling heat.

Nights of no sleep leave time for my mind to wander and wonder. Were these changes going to happen on their own, or were they pushed along by perimenopause? Are these changes I'm navigating, or is it more of an evolution? I prefer the latter when I think about the meaning of change versus evolution. By choosing to evolve I feel like I have a say in what is happening and how and why. I'm in the driver's seat. Change, meanwhile, has a feeling of things happening *to* me and not necessarily for me. Things that aren't necessarily part of my life plan.

Learning to trust and open up to friends, creating intimacy with those older than me and who have already travelled the menopause path, means receiving the most incredible gifts of support and advice. Their willingness to share their stories and experiences has made me so much less afraid of what lies ahead. There is light at the end of the tunnel.

Learning to open myself up more is an experience, and as I get older, it's getting easier. I am learning that the opinions of others are not a true value of my worth. Their reaction to me and my truth only reflects themselves and their issues.

At this point, there is one certainty: navigating intimacy is a life-long journey. You never arrive at an endpoint because there isn't one. There is no destination. The journey continues deeper, layered and more nuanced. There is only growth and understanding and acceptance. I find comfort in knowing that there isn't a target, that there is no test or final exam, it's simply ongoing. I don't have to be perfect; I just have to be open to learning and exploring and growing.

Losing My Religion
(to Find My Divinity)

BY BEAR PHILLIPS

Content: childhood sexual abuse, sexual shame, BDSM and kink, power dynamics, anal penetration, healing through intimacy

PART I

How could reality ever live up to a fantasy? The thought was foremost in my mind as the door to a new, cookie-cutter flat, overlooking the wastelands of East London, inched open.

I had been drawn to this point – of want and desire – repeatedly for years, but never before had I acted on it.

My desire felt so shameful. And it had been with me for years...

To surrender. To be taken.

By a woman...

With a strap-on.

These days, strap-on sex is one of the top searches on PornHub (experimenting with sex and sexuality a much more accepted and even celebrated pastime), but at the turn of the century, titles on old VHS tapes such as *Bend Over Boyfriend*, were only just beginning to leave their mark on the collective psyche.

I didn't know of the *Bend Over Boyfriend* phenomenon back then. I had only known a fascination with the pleasures of my own bottom, matched by a crippling shame, and a self-destructive impulse: If I was to give in to this sickening sexual urge, as I believed it to be, then I would take myself down in the process.

This would not end well. How could it…?

* * *

What I did not want to acknowledge was the beginnings of this desire.

What I could not fully face was my younger self; on all fours, as a child, locked behind the bathroom door as bath time with my father unfolded.

I wasn't raped. At least not that I can remember. And not if the narrow definition is to have been penetrated by a penis.

For years, into my 30s, this simple fact made it difficult for me to even comprehend that I had experienced childhood sexual abuse at the hands of my father.

What I experienced was so much more complicated than that.

Bath times were perhaps the only times I felt close to the man. Intimate. Connected even, in the heat and the steam and the skin-on-skin closeness.

His was a naive and immature sexuality – one which later made sense as I pieced together the puzzle of my father's line, and the abuse that began with my father's father. *His* story being a Salvation Army minister, returning from the horrors of World War I, where his contribution to the Allied effort had been to read Last Rights to the dismembered and dying on the blood and mud-hewn fields of Flanders.

My father, for his part, was part of the Raj in India, still a teenager as the Second World War gathered pace in the East.

I would later reflect on how the seams of colonialism, patriarchy, and trauma run deep in me.

"No one talks about how the sexual revolution started in the '50s," my father would say, with a nudge and a wink, his atheist playboy world at odds with my mother's deeply religious views. As a child, I was caught in the turbulence between their many irreconcilable views on love and life.

And as I awakened to the physical sensations that my body could afford me – a whole new playground of unexpected and unexplored delights – so too did my mother's sense of shame descend on me like a cloud.

I remember being naked under the bedclothes, my five-year-old self revelling at the feel and touch of the sheet against my bare skin, my jim-jams on the chair still, as my mother sat on the edge of the bed to tuck me in.

In my mind's eye the lights dim to black, my body laid out, hands by my sides, rigid beneath the sheet. A death shroud for little me.

With the dimming of my light, I knew – without a doubt – how broken I was.

* * *

The thing with childhood abuse of any kind is the loss of the self.

When an adult is using you to satisfy his or her own needs, what they do not see is the autonomous human being in front of them. In that moment, our only purpose for existing is to serve someone else's needs.

Our self-hood is erased.

Gabor Maté talks about the different types of traumas

we may experience in our lives: the capital-T Trauma of those who suffer PTSD following extreme life events, or the little-t trauma that so many suffer on a daily basis, especially if marginalised by society.

But he also references the experience of the trauma we may hold in our young bodies, of what perhaps *should* have happened, but didn't.

So, despite the inner voices screaming at me about how disgusting I was to be paying someone to have my fantasies realised, the intention to claim them as my own, to own them – if only for the briefest moment – pressed me on. Because, despite the shame, I was engaged in a deeply profound moment of personal agency: *My* choice. *My* decision.

My desire...

Yet, how could reality ever live up to the fantasy my mind had conjured for so many years?

* * *

To this day I remember the moment with extraordinary clarity. The well-lubed dildo searching for the way in, assertive yet going nowhere. I remember murmured words, turning my head toward the sound...

And there it was.

Presence!

The gift of a human being offering me her complete and undivided attention.

In that moment I felt as though I was the only person in the world who mattered.

Under the wide-eyed gaze of this human being, attuned to my every breath, my every heartbeat, I opened.

I welcomed her in.

Feeling her hands on my back and on my hips.

The tip of her cock touched something deep inside my being.

The pleasure was a rapture.

My whole life I had understood God to be this judgemental All-Knowing and All-Seeing force, outside of and above me, casting judgement and finding me wanting at every turn. But now, here it was – touched with pleasure – a lotus flower blossoming within me. The divinity within. Deep inside my body.

How could a bundle of skin and muscle and bone, capable of experiencing this amount of exquisite pleasure, possibly be wrong?

Through the blur of body parts and positions, I felt the tension I had been carrying my whole life fall away under her watchful and attentive gaze. I arrived back in my embodied self, no longer separate and divided, no longer outside of my Self.

✳ ✳ ✳

Gabor makes a profoundly important assertion: that the healing of our trauma can only begin when the conditions for safety are met.

And what is safety? I understood that day that safety is the full presence and awareness that we can bring to each other. A sacred holding, and the holding of the sacred. It is the holding we may have never experienced as children – fully accepted for who we are, without judgement, and with a sense of awe for the potentials and possibilities we might bring to the world.

I am this possibility coming to fruition. There will never be another me, having lived this particular life, with this particular set of learnings and wisdom, just as there will never be another you. *Your* uniqueness is to be cultivated and cherished.

I was offered an extraordinary gift that day. A seed was planted that I might in turn be able to hold others, with my full presence, my full acceptance, and my awe at the possibilities for wholeness and healing that we each carry inside of us, moving like seedlings arching toward the sun.

PART II

As we disentangled and embraced, I pulled her toward me, lost in the pleasure of skin, and flesh, my fingers gently but firmly kneading her shoulders, her back.

"I see you..." she said, giving me a playful but sideways look, "there's more going on here than meets the eye!"

And she was right.

She was a Dominatrix, and yes, what I had experienced was a deeply submissive act – one that I think all men should experience, at least once in their lives.

But that was also a problem. My submission was, for me, also a way of being in my life. I had submitted to another's whims and desires from my earliest years, and in later life had played the role of the good son, the dutiful husband, and the loving father figure.

But what of it had ever come about through my choice and volition? How much of it had been my people-pleasing to keep those around me happy, and to keep myself safe?

Where had I ever really chosen to live my life on my terms?

* * *

The question of power is at the heart of kink and BDSM. Even more so in the world of conscious kink, where we might bring our full attention to what is happening – and what we might want to happen – within pre-agreed and mutually consenting boundaries.

Because of this, my explorations in this subculture have helped me develop a sensitivity to power dynamics. I've come to appreciate how (from moment to moment), the power can shift within a single conversation. How a raised eyebrow or the most subtle change in voice can skew the dynamic between two people in an ongoing and ever-shifting dance – a tango if you will in which the roles of leader and follower might swap in the blink of an eye. I now have a greater awareness of how power dynamics play out in the world at large, in our institutions and political systems, those structures of power we so often take for granted.

But the possibility of claiming my power was beginning to take up residence in my psyche. It had not yet been articulated so succinctly – to begin with, it was more the frustrations at my lack of personal agency, my sovereignty, in the face of a lifetime of anxious people-pleasing.

Yet here I was, months after our first encounter, after sessions where I had been offered the reins of power – gifted the flogger or paddle – but been simply unable to connect with that power inside myself...

Here I was with a burning flame tracing the line of my spine. In that moment, my Domme was an artist with her brush, creating me in her image.

As the fire in one hand set my body alight, the flame hovering above my skin, her other hand put the fire out in a series of strokes that released the energy coiled at the base of my spine, flicking it away at the top of my neck. Old, sticky and tar-like energy, melting and giving way to something new and pure.

With every stroke, my body undulated. The energy grew. Building. A rumble deep in my belly. Shifting imperceptibly into a growl.

I have no memory of rising, but the image seared in my

mind is of kneeling at the very edge of the massage table, my fists clenched by my sides, every muscle in my being twisted and torqued, the rumble of a growl expanding into a full-throated roar!

Power as a visceral experience; it lay there like the sweat in the pores of my skin, filling me completely.

And yet... There was a very clear edge! The edge of that massage table felt like the lip of a precipice. I could roar to my heart's content, but the brink was immediate – I could see how easy it would be to cross that line and fall into the void.

But there, in that moment, I experienced the fullness that was possible by coming right up to that edge.

I found my power that day. I experienced the possibility of power within limits, and that perhaps the experience of power was all the stronger for the boundary that contained it. I discovered that power and strength could be wielded with safety.

I was gifted the embodied knowing that I could be powerful *and* safe in my sexuality. Rather than the shy, awkward, full-of-shame man I had grown to become, stealing sideways glances, my unmet desires and needs seeping out in my awkward interactions with those I was attracted to, I came to realise I could own my sexuality. Fully. I could own my wants and needs, in the full knowledge of that edge and limit I had experienced.

I think of it now, still using the metaphor of fire. I think of it in the sense that many men use their sexuality like a flame-thrower, burning anyone and anything that might lie within reach of their gaze, desperate in their wanting. I set that against the vision of a lantern within which the fire can grow, with intensity, giving of its light, warmth, and heat, yet safely contained; drawing other beings towards its radiance.

PART III

I consider myself to be a "loving Dominant" and, in my work and personal life, work with what I call my *Daddy* energy.

Let me remind you that kink is the intentional role-playing and conscious power exchange between consenting adults.

When I call myself a Daddy, what I am referring to here is the energy of loving nurturance. It can extend into sexual play, again within the bounds of two or more adults consenting to do so, but fundamentally, for me, it is about an attitude of care. Of attentiveness. Even of unconditional love.

When I work with my clients, the experience of unconditional love becomes possible precisely because of the boundaries, container, and safety of the session. It is the most profound privilege to be able to witness the transformations in others that are possible when we can simply "be" with each other.

I not only get to offer others the presence and attunement that I experienced that grey day in East London, but I get to experience for myself – first-hand – the holding and accepting father energy I had never known.

I feel blessed that I get to heal my own masculine and father wounds by providing for others the safe container and the safe holding that I did not know in my own childhood. I feel blessed that I get to model for others that it is possible to be a safe man in the world. One who is not denuded and desexualised, but fully in touch with his deepest desires and ever-evolving fantasies – at peace with the knowledge that the reality of our lives can be better than we may ever imagine.

Sensitive Single Seeks Sexy Soulmate

BY JENNIFER COCKCROFT

Content: *chronic illness, medical examination, celibacy, online dating, penetration*

I lay back on the bed, my legs spread wide, a sheet of paper towel almost useless at protecting any sense of modesty, as the nurse bent over and tried to insert the speculum.

I tensed at the intrusion.

Her voice came from between my legs, "Oh, you're quite tight, aren't you?" A statement more than a question. "Have you had children?" she asked.

I shook my head before realising that she couldn't see me from where she was, then replied, "No."

More wiggling and pushing that made my body want to twist away.

"And when was the last time you had sex?" The question was asked with such detachment as if she wasn't really interested in hearing the answer as she tried valiantly to complete the smear test.

Except it wasn't just an idle question to me.

I went still.

It only took a couple of seconds to do the maths.

"2008."

"Oh!" the nurse exclaimed, banging her head on the overhead light that was illuminating my nether regions as she stood up in surprise.

The last time I had sex was fifteen years ago. The distraction of this realisation was enough to temporarily disconnect my brain from the rest of my body so that the nurse could quickly finish what she was doing, finally sending me on my way with a blush of embarrassment on her face.

I'm pretty sure that if I'd looked in the mirror there would have been absolutely no colour in my face whatsoever. Everything had been drained away by the quiet shock of acknowledging that a decade and a half of my life had passed by without any kind of sexual intimacy with another human being.

I mean it's not like I'd never thought about it in all that time.

Wanted it.

I had.

A lot.

I'd consider myself a healthy woman with healthy desires and a healthy libido. But apparently, rather than offering me opportunities to satisfy those desires, life and circumstances and the relentless passage of time had other ideas for me.

In fact, if you look back at the major events of those fifteen years since my last relationship (okay, fine, my only ever relationship, but that's another story entirely) it makes for pretty miserable reading.

I lost three of my grandparents in that time and had taken on caring responsibilities for two of them during their deteriorating illnesses. And then once the actual bereavements occurred, I was caught in the middle of not only the emotional grief but the administrative complications of settling estates too.

My jobs during those years became overwhelmingly stressful – working in retail during an economic crisis is not for the faint-hearted – and I changed roles every couple of years, trying to find something that made me feel better.

But they didn't, and that led to niggling aches that developed into chronic pain, alongside worsening mental health and episodes of burnout and depression. A cocktail of appointments with physiotherapists, osteopaths, mindfulness classes, talking therapy and medication offered some short-term relief but also left me feeling as though my mind, body, and soul were constantly at war with one another.

All these things took up so much of my time and energy and I had very little left over to be able to contemplate a social life, let alone a love life. Not that there was much chance of either: I had few local friends, always worked in teams of other women, and had no spare money to go anywhere or do anything that might introduce me to new people or potential partners.

And so, the years marched on, and any connection with my sexual self remained hidden, and mostly ignored except in secret moments of self-pleasure.

I said I was a woman with healthy desires, and that remains true.

I still find random men in the street attractive. Have a few major crushes on celebrities. Read as many steamy romance novels as my Kindle can handle, with my favourite scenes bookmarked so I can go back to them again and again. Watch romantic and sexy movies. And yes, even dabble in a bit of online porn on occasion.

I know the things that turn me on, and I know ways to get myself off.

Mainly with the help of a small battery-powered vibrator that I hide under a pile of blankets in the drawer under my bed (even though no one besides me is ever likely to find it) and bring out in the dark of night, under the covers, when I need the physical release of a quick orgasm.

Because that's all they are. Quickies. A pressure valve to relieve tension.

All the foreplay happens in my head, my imagination doing all the work of arousing my body, until I just need a little help with the big finish.

Which is very much not how I want to experience a real-life sex life.

I mean sure, adventurous thoughts of one-night stands cross my mind on occasion, but I know deep down that I likely wouldn't be able to keep things purely physical. I need an emotional connection. An intellectual and spiritual one too. To feel a broader and deeper sense of intimacy with someone that grows through conversation and spending time together. Allowing an attraction to build to the point where I can't *not* expose my whole self to them, to trust them with my body and my feelings, and know that they feel the same.

Wishful thinking? Maybe. But all that sexy romantic fiction has given me high standards and expectations, and I refuse to apologise for that.

Anyway, since that appointment and the slightly terrifying reminder about how quickly time is passing, I haven't been able to stop thinking about meeting someone and breaking my record celibacy stint. About finding the love of my life. About not ending up as a weird, lonely spinster.

And, as it seems to be the best option given my circumstances and the way of this 21st-century world, I've decided to brave the wilds of online dating.

Wish me luck.

* * *

What a minefield.

First, there's choosing which app to download from a myriad of options, all of which appear to promise unique matching algorithms, more matches than anyone else, and different ways of showing your appreciation for potential partners. Not to mention the different energies, from pure hook-ups to speciality interests – and that could be anything from board games to BDSM.

Then there's crafting your profile. What on earth do you say?! How do you share enough but not too much, come across as approachable but not weird, be funny and sassy but not a total slut, say what you're looking for but not put off any man that comes near you?

And don't even get me started on the photos.

Fortunately, most of the apps let you edit your profile easily and as often as you like, and I definitely take advantage of that feature, tweaking my personal bio and adjusting my answers to the dreaded icebreaker questions. Again, these run the gamut from basic to cheesy to downright provocative.

I get the usual slew of spammy matches and unpleasant invitations, all of which are deleted instantly. Eventually, things settle down, and I even have a few conversations with potential men that sadly don't go anywhere.

I'm careful not to obsess over this. Because I know how easily I can get completely absorbed in something until it takes over my life.

And actually, I don't want finding a partner to be all

that defines me. I still want to be me as an individual, with my own likes and dislikes and things that I do. But it would be really nice to add a romantic relationship into the mix. In the meantime, I still have my smutty novels, my vibrator, and my very vivid imagination.

I begin to reconnect to my physicality too. Touching myself. And not just in an erotic way. I pay more attention to how my fingers feel on my face when I smear on moisturiser in the morning. To the slip and slide of flannel and soap on my limbs in the shower. The way the earth feels under my feet when I go barefoot in the garden. The stretch and tension of muscles when I move – and the aches and pains when I move too much!

Getting to know my body again in little everyday ways, which then naturally progress into more intimate explorations. Figuring out what brings me pleasure. And what kind of pleasure. Deciding I want more of all of it.

* * *

It's the age-old question. How much do you share about yourself on a first date? Or before the first meeting when you're chatting online? I've experimented with being direct from the beginning, and with waiting until it becomes relevant to the conversation. So far, I haven't had much success with either.

Of course, having it scare them off from the get-go is an easy way of weeding out the duds, but then when you think you're starting to build a good connection, you tell him, and then he runs away, that's not a fun feeling.

Oh, and maybe I should have been clear – I'm not talking about sexual preferences here, I'm talking about disclosing a chronic illness that has an impact on everyday life.

Exhibit A: the guy who decided that he couldn't be with

a woman who couldn't keep up with his extreme sports habit – despite never having mentioned such an interest anywhere previously – and cut the date short before we even got to dessert.

I stayed and ate one anyway, and the restaurant gave it to me for free after seeing his abrupt exit. It was delicious. I moaned in pleasure at the first mouthful. Out loud. In public.

I'm beginning to find the whole dating thing exhausting. Tedious. And a little bit soul-destroying.

Why are none of the men in real life like the book boyfriends I swoon over?

And then I meet him.

* * *

For a start, he's actually happy to chat via text for more than five minutes without immediately suggesting meeting up. Big tick.

And his texts are written in proper sentences, with excellent spelling, grammar, and punctuation, and just a few intentionally chosen emojis. Perfect. Condemn me all you want, but this girl gets hot for a man with an above-average command of the English language.

He also asks questions that come across as genuine interest, covering a broad range of subjects, as well as offering considered answers of his own. Gold star.

So, by the time we arrange to meet for lunch one weekend – it feels less pressured than a big evening date – I'm feeling hopeful, with giddy butterflies in my belly.

And, oh boy, he does not disappoint.

Rather endearingly, he seems just as nervous as me when we first meet. There's a sweet fumble over whether we go for a handshake, hug, or cheek kiss that helps break the ice with mutual laughter. And after that, we get on like a house on fire.

Lunch turns into the entire afternoon, first ensconced in a lovely café, and then continuing with an aimless walk once the staff start giving us pointed looks about how long we've been taking up the table.

I feel... everything... around him. Comfortable and safe, inspired and challenged, intellectually alive and physically aroused. Desperately attracted to the irresistible combination of looks and personality, flattered by his attention and the old-fashioned, gentlemanly manners that have him opening doors, helping me into my coat, and walking on the road side of the pavement to keep me away from the traffic.

We talk about so much, the conversation flowing so effortlessly that I honestly couldn't tell you how we got onto the subject of my health. The combination of conditions I'd finally – after what felt like endless tests and consultations – received formal diagnoses of in the last couple of years, and how they affect my daily life.

He listens.

Without judgement.

With curiosity and openness to my experiences.

With questions about what he can do to help when we see each other again.

Because obviously, we will.

I think I fall in love with him right there and then.

***

While the intellectual and emotional side of our relationship develops quickly and incredibly easily, the physical side of things is... well it takes a little while to find our way together.

Which, in a way, is a good thing. A really good thing.

The waiting builds the anticipation, attraction, and arousal to such a level that once we finally get there, it truly is every cliché of bone-melting and earth-shattering satisfaction you could dream of.

Getting there is a bumpy ride though. There are moments of awkwardness and overthinking, trying to work out which positions work best for us both, his exquisite care and attention reaching the point of annoying when I just want – *need* – more. Harder. Faster. Deeper. There. Right... there.

Fortunately, we're able to laugh about it together, and to work out how to communicate when something feels good or not, when I need to shift to be more comfortable, and to stop him panicking every time my body erupts into a symphony of occasionally shocking sound effects.

Pretty much every joint in my body is capable of some fairly spectacular pops, cracks, crunches, clunks, and even the odd partial dislocation. The first time I woke him in the night because of a slipped rib he'd thought I was having a heart attack from the way I described the pain radiating round my torso. And honestly, I'd thought the same the first time it happened to me. A bit of stretching usually does the trick of settling it back into place, but his knuckles gently massaging the tension from the muscles was a very pleasurable bonus.

My muscles, tendons and ligaments don't always work quite the way they're supposed to either, meaning that while I'm very flexible, I'm also prone to random cramping and spasms, as well as post-exertional pain and fatigue.

Oh, and I bruise really easily too.

The first morning we wake up to a set of perfect but livid purple fingerprints on my thighs after some impassioned grabbing the night before, he's so guilty and apologetic he barely touches me at all for days.

I have to take matters into my own hands to persuade him that I'm fine. That sometimes the bruises are worth it. And not his fault, when I almost constantly have patches in varying shades of yellow, green and blue dotting my skin from accidentally knocking or walking into things.

His patience seems to know no bounds, and once he understands that spontaneous sex isn't always going to be an option, we're able to make the times we do have together really count.

Pacing and managing my energy levels are a big part of how I have to schedule my time – making sure I'm rested before work days, or any big appointments or events, and giving myself plenty of recovery time afterwards. Breaks during are often a regular feature too.

That's not to say we don't fit in the odd fast and frantic session when I'm having a good day, or times when he takes the lead, encouraging me to lie back and relax. Although how I'm supposed to relax when he goes down on me with such devastating skill and enthusiasm that every nerve ending in my body feels connected to my clit as I climax in an explosion of fireworks, I'm not quite sure.

Remember how I said that most of my solo foreplay had been the imaginary kind? Well, with him, foreplay is one of my favourite parts.

When we have the time to explore every inch of each other in infinite detail, for no millimetre of skin to go untouched, unkissed, unawakened, we each discover erogenous zones we didn't know were there.

And that knowledge gives us power.

The power to reduce each other to a trembling, turned-on mess in a heartbeat.

Not that I complain about that very often.

And it means that even the smaller, everyday interactions have a frisson to them. When his warm breath hits my neck as he nips at my earlobe. When I scrape my nails through the short hairs at his nape. When his strong arms wrap tightly around my waist as he hugs me from behind. When my hands fall to the waistband of his trousers and make his abs clench.

And when I struggle to get in or out of my clothes because of the pain, the way his touch brushes against my ribs while he does up the clasp of my bra, a promise of greater pleasure when he strips it from me again later.

Some days I don't want anything, let alone him, to touch me at all. But some days being anchored against his body, enfolded in his arms, is the only thing that keeps me from falling apart.

That's the thing with my conditions. The unpredictability. Even with all the measures I take to manage my symptoms, I never really know when something is going to flare up, how long it will take to heal – or if it'll even get better at all.

He takes all this change a lot better than I do, going with the flow and adapting while I get frustrated and fight back.

Last week was a prime example.

I was cooking dinner, happily pottering in the kitchen, and daydreaming about a few days previous when we'd had an impromptu kitchen disco because a playlist of some of our favourite songs had come on the radio, sending us into fits of giggles as we tried to remember 20-year-old dance routines. Eventually, we'd given up and he'd swung me into a searing kiss, lifting me up to sit on the counter and stepping between my legs.

Unfortunately, the distraction of remembering what had followed was enough for me not to be fully paying attention as I went to lift the pan full of simmering Bolognese. I lost my grip, sending the whole thing crashing to the floor, the noise of which brought him running.

"Hey, are you okay?" his first question. Always, his first thoughts are for me, with never a hint of blame or anger at the mess.

I must have nodded numbly, because he pulled me over to sit at the table, my hands in his as he knelt, ducking his head to find my eyes where I was trying to avoid looking at him.

"Yeah... I... my wrist gave way," I whispered, and instantly his warm fingers began a gentle, soothing massage.

Dropping a swift kiss on my palm, he pushed to his feet again, moving to collect paper towels, cleaning spray and a mop to clean the red splatter from all over the floor. I glanced over to see the pan with a huge dent now deforming the base, and the handle at a strange angle where it had landed and bounced.

As I sat there watching him, this wonderful man, cleaning up the mess I'd made without complaint, tears filled my eyes and my inner gremlins emerged to play.

"I'm so sorry," I managed to get out, "I wasn't paying attention, and I know that pan's heavy... so stupid..." The tears started to fall, and I struggled to breathe between the sobs working their way up my chest.

He was back in front of me in seconds, kneeling close, thumbs reaching to wipe the tears from my cheeks. "Hey, hey, it's fine, no harm done, it's only a pan." He tipped my chin to meet his gaze, quirking a half smile.

Normally his patience and understanding made me smile too, but right then it had the opposite effect.

"But I hate this! I hate that I always end up breaking things, or making a mess, or hurting myself!" I cried, frustration bringing colour to my face. "I hate that life feels so hard, and I don't understand why you don't hate it too. Why you're not angry with me for ruining dinner. I don't understand why you stay with me when my stupid broken body makes everything so difficult! I don't want you to end up being my carer!"

Now my eyes were blazing, holding his, daring him to respond.

He paused for a moment, something flicking across his face that was too quick for me to read.

"You want me to be angry?" he replied quietly, too calmly for my liking. I nodded once. "Okay, I am angry. And I do hate this," he continued, "but I'm not angry at you," his tone softened, "I'm angry that you have to go through this. I hate that I can't take the pain away. It frustrates me constantly that I can't make it better. But I'm not leaving you. I love you." My heart squeezed like it always did when he said those three little words. "All of you. And you're not broken. Sure, your body does some weird and wonderful things sometimes," another one of those smiles at this attempt to lighten the mood, "but it just makes you special. And even more beautiful. And yes, I want to take care of you and make sure you never get hurt, but more than that I want to be with you and figure things out together, to get to see how strong and amazing you are, to experience the highs and the lows with you. Because I love you."

Well, when he made a speech like that, was it any surprise that I dissolved into a fresh flood of tears?

Flinging my arms around him, I held as tight as I could, my face buried in his neck. He managed to manoeuvre us so that he was sitting on the chair with me cradled in his lap, his arms around me, one hand stroking my back as the sobs gradually slowed.

When I was finally able to lift my head and meet his eyes again, I shaped my face into a wobbly smile and cupped his jaw with one hand.

"What did I do to deserve you?" I hiccupped out between shaky breaths. "You're too good to me. But I'm so glad you're not planning on going anywhere, because I love you too, so much."

His kiss was sweet and gentle, and I returned it, trying to pour all my gratitude into the moment.

"So," he said, when he lifted his head again, "takeaway for dinner then?"

All I could do was swat at his teasing grin and laugh.

* * *

He got me the best present I've ever received for Christmas this year.

A body pillow.

One of those ones that wraps all the way around in a loop to support as many joints as possible in the optimum comfortable position.

I know, I know, it doesn't exactly sound like the most exciting, or sexiest, gift ever, and it's the butt of many a joke to give or receive household goods, but trust me, he really couldn't have got me anything better.

As much as we both love falling asleep together, waking together spooned into each other, we've also discovered over time that we have very different sleep styles. He can sleep like the dead while the slightest noise will wake me. He snores; I move around a lot. He's always hot and I wear socks in bed nine months of the year.

So, we've been experimenting with sleeping in separate

beds most nights of the week. That way we both stand a chance of getting the rest we need, for him to cope with his job and for me to just get through the day.

Hence the body pillow.

And, oh my heavens what a difference it's made! My body can finally relax while feeling fully supported, and I don't have to worry about elbowing him in the ribs if I need to turn over.

Trying it out for the first time was the best sleep I've had in absolutely ages.

Every time I wake up feeling refreshed and with my aches reduced to their lowest level, I want to celebrate that fact. With him.

I pad across to his room, pausing in the doorway to admire the view. He's on his back, the covers pushed down to his waist revealing the muscular planes of his torso, dusted with hair that arrows down over his belly, gently rising and falling with each slow breath.

One arm is outstretched as if beckoning to me, so I crawl onto the mattress towards him, tucking myself into the warmth of his side. Even in sleep, he feels the movement and his arm wraps around my back, his face turning towards me, breathing deep into my hair.

I let my fingers dance over the constellation of freckles that scatter his skin, following them down his chest and stomach, feeling the muscles tremble at the light touch.

His eyes flicker open as he sighs deeply, finally coming awake. I lever myself up so that my chin rests on his chest and my face is the first thing he sees.

"G'morning," his voice is thick and deeper than normal.

"Good morning," I smile as he blinks a couple more times to bring me into focus.

"You okay?" he asks. "Sleep well?" Now he's sweeping

soft strokes up and down my back sending sparks along my spine.

"Mmmm, really well," I reply, my smile wider, and my hand wandering further down, diving beneath the covers to the ridges and dips of muscle that direct me from his hips towards his groin.

A hissed intake of breath tells me he's paying me complete attention now. His eyes flare and his smile turns wicked.

"Oh really? How well?"

I shuffle higher so that my mouth is just inches from his.

"So well, I think I ought to kiss you to say thank you again for the pillow."

He rolls us both to our sides, his mouth meeting mine, and drawing my leg over his hip so that I can feel the heat and growing hardness of him against my centre.

His hands work fast but with such tenderness as he removes the vest and shorts that I wear to sleep in until we're skin to skin.

Not wanting to rush my thank you, I let my fingers explore everywhere I can reach, and his do the same, awakening my body into a tingling mass of nerve endings.

I gasp when his hand delves between my legs, and he growls his appreciation at the wet slickness that meets him.

The shoulder I'm lying on makes its presence felt with a vicious crunch, so I push against his chest to roll him to his back again.

"Sit up," I whisper the command, and it only takes a second for his answering smile to tell me he knows what I have in mind.

Readjusting himself so he can lean back against the headboard, and dealing with protection in the process, I climb onto his lap, this time my hip clunking in protest as I straddle him.

I drop my forehead to his, nose tips touching, and let out a sound that's half groan, half chuckle. He meets it with a soft kiss, one hand cupping my face, the thumb stroking over my cheek, the other resting softly on the offending hip.

"Okay?" he asks again, an icy flash of concern tempering the flames of desire in his eyes.

I nod and smile. "I'm fine, promise." And I kiss him back.

With his legs butterflied to support me, mine circle around him. As I lower myself to take him in, I purr at the exquisite sensation of being filled, my inner muscles stretching and relaxing to accommodate him. He lets out a groan as I sink down fully, his head bowed against my chest, arms wrapped around my back to anchor us completely together.

For a few seconds, we simply sit there, breathing, savouring the closeness.

When he teasingly traces his fingers from my hips, up either side of my waist and ribcage, and then down my back, it sets off a shower of tingles that has me arching against him, clenching down on him, the pleasure all beginning to gather in my pelvis like a bowl of pure, molten desire.

As I squeeze him within me, it elicits a rumble that vibrates through his whole body, and I feel him try to thrust further, higher, but limited by our position.

I continue to rock and circle my hips, grasping his shoulders for support and whimpering as I find an angle that strokes exactly the right spot.

His breaths grow shorter, thighs tensing harder beneath mine, arms holding me tighter to his chest, and I know he's as close as I am.

The warmth spreads. The tension builds. Yet at the same time, it feels like my entire body is becoming boneless and the most relaxed I've ever been.

His mouth claims mine again as we both strain to reach the peak together. I think I stop breathing as I approach my climax, knowing he's right there with me. Just... a... little... bit... more...

❊ ❊ ❊

Blinking away the daydream I look back down at the phone in my hands, the dating profile I've been carefully crafting for the last hour waiting for me to hit the 'publish' button.

Am I really ready for this?

To try it for real?

Quite apart from the prospect of facing that question from a nurse again, I know I don't want to be alone. I know I want to explore all the possibilities of intimacy and pleasure. And not just on my own.

I know there will be challenges, but I'm willing to face them.

My thumb hovers.

Okay. Here goes.

Lightening Up:
Adventures in Self-liberation

BY ESTHER LEMMENS

Content: *gender identity, gender roles, sexual identity, neurodivergence, self-discovery*

*"The only way to deal with an unfree world
is to become so absolutely free that your very
existence is an act of rebellion."*

– Albert Camus

I've always loved the idea of my very existence being an act of rebellion. It feels fierce and powerful. Funny when you realise that after half a century on the planet, you couldn't be further from it. Half a century. *Five decades.* For some reason, the latter makes more sense. I can break down what happened in a decade. I'm able to get a feel for what it contained.

In my twenties and thirties, I had a lot of fun exploring sex and intimacy, pushing the boundaries of what is vanilla a little bit more with each relationship. I considered myself quite sexually liberated, even though for the most part (with a few exceptions), I had mono-cis-het (monogamous, cisgender, and heterosexual) sex. I learned about my body, had a healthy sexual appetite, and I knew how to orgasm. Meaning, how to *make* myself orgasm in response to a lover's touch. I found my lover's arousal a turn-on, and sex, for me, was a sensory feast; a blend of skin-to-skin touch, pressure, intensity, movement, rhythm... A delicious way of being embodied.

In my forties, everything changed. I was about to have an awakening of sorts; one that was enlightening as well as challenging.

As opposed to just one, there were multiple wake-up calls; meeting a trans non-binary person who would become my partner, making friends with many more gender-expansive folks following that, having more queer relationships, starting a podcast sharing conversations with some of said folks and many others all over the world, and working on becoming a better ally to my LGBTQIA+ siblings. Oh, and starting to embrace everything quirky and wonderful about me – and everything not quite so wonderful (that's a bit more challenging, it turns out).

Being a naturally curious person, diving into sex, gender, and sexuality was fascinating and delightful. It has opened my eyes in unexpected ways. And through learning about other folks, I learned about myself, too. I became more self-aware and started to get a more complete idea of the society I live and grew up in. Even though my motto for life is 'question everything' (something that most authority figures do not appreciate all that much, I've learned), I'd been blind to a lot of it until then. It's been a confusing and expansive ride.

As much as my body changed in my forties, the biggest change was not an outside change, but an inside one; real-ising and accepting that I am not the person I thought I was, and the world is not as I thought it was. My idea of the world may still not be any more accurate than before I had this epiphany, but it's my experience, and that's what I have to work with.

Life is filtered through our experiences. What we hear is not necessarily the same as what is said to us; even if you speak the same language, a single word can have different meanings to different people.

Take the word 'sex'. What I experience as sex isn't necessarily what someone else experiences as sex. Being allosexual (experiencing sexual attraction), pansexual (attracted to genders of all sorts), AFAB (assigned female at birth), a woman, queer, neurodivergent, an intuitive, and a highly sensitive person, are all facets of my identity that contribute to how I understand and experience sex.

Then there are my past experiences of relating to others, how I was conditioned, and how I've been in the world – they also contribute to how I understand and experience sex.

I had fallen into the romance trap; this idealised story of how relationships *should* start, escalate, and 'end up', plus the acceptable steps towards this fairy-tale goal.

Romantic (hetero)sexual relationships are seen as the gold standard of relationships; anything else is just not good enough. Friendships are great, but they don't qualify as 'real' relationships. Platonic relationships with emotional intimacy? Also no. If there isn't a penis going into a vagina, it doesn't seem to count.

Society dictates not just that we are all sexual beings, but that we are sexual beings who want to actively and enthusiastically share that with others, in ways that are also dictated by said society.

If you have a penis, you're expected to want to use it to penetrate, as often as possible, and to enjoy that more than anything else in life. Being a stud is the aim.

If you have a vagina, however... Okay, you're allowed to enjoy being penetrated (because not wanting that is completely unacceptable), but also not too much because then you're a slut. And you're allowed to have a libido, but not too high (definitely not higher than the man who's penetrating you) because then shame on you. Also, whether you enjoy it or not doesn't really matter, but you must be sexually available to your man any time he wants. That's your marital duty.

This, apparently, is 'normal'. So normal that everyone seems to accept it for what it is, without question. It can be difficult to put words to all this, but once you do, the dysfunction lights up like those fluorescent lights in an old office block; they hurt my eyes and make me feel ill.

Being on the vagina-owner side of the equation, to say I've had enough of this bullshit is an understatement. I mean, sure, I've had some great sex, some not-so-great sex, and everything in between, in my twenties and thirties. However, soon after I entered my forties, things slowed down. I became perimenopausal, and my partner came out as asexual, so our sexual relationship went on early retirement. Truly, a chicken-or-the-egg situation. Was my libido waning because I wasn't having sex? Or was I not having (and wanting) as much sex because my libido had gone on holiday? Or a combination of both?

(I still don't know the answer to that question.)

I wondered, did it even matter? Because answer or no answer, I was where I was. My sexuality disappeared into hibernation, I felt like the gap between me and that part of me was growing ever bigger, and I didn't know what to do about it.

So, I focused on other things. Creative ideas. I mean, that's a similar energy, right? Sacral. Sexual. Creative.

Expressive. If I'm not making love, I can make art instead.

For a while, my enthusiasm seemed to soothe the lost-ness by providing sparks of creative joy. But it became more and more evident I needed to rekindle that part of myself. I felt like my sexuality, my femininity, was slowly losing its colour, fading to grey. Even though having an open relationship had been on the table since I met my partner, establishing and maintaining new intimate relationships felt like an insurmountable quest, and I'd never felt further from being a passionate, pleasure-seeking, sexual being.

Eventually, I made peace with the sexual spark of my relationship burning out, and we agreed that if/when I was ready to explore other routes of getting my sexual needs met, I would say so, and we would talk about it.

My partner coming out as asexual was part of their identity journey: being AMAB (assigned male at birth) trans non-binary, and weighing up whether or not to have gender-affirming surgery. Although I was missing sexual intimacy, I was happy that my partner felt safe enough in our relationship to come out as asexual; to finally own up to what didn't feel good to them, and to draw a line under it.

Not too long after coming out as asexual, my part-ner's surgery solidified as an actual date on the calendar. They were still reluctant about it, but the pros (just) out-weighed the cons. I had my own theory: *if you don't use it, you won't miss it*. It seemed simple; since we hadn't been having (penetrative) sex, the pressure to keep performing in that way dissolved. So, no need to hold on to an obsolete appendage.

This was my first relationship with a gender-expansive person, and in a new wave of liberation, I embraced my queerness and being pansexual (feeling attracted to any and all genders) on a new level. Later in my forties, I started having other queer relationships, including with trans, non-binary, and asexual (ace) folks.

After further sexplorations with asexual folks (some not knowing they were ace, but trying to live up to societal expectations, like my partner was) I was fascinated to realise that having sex with someone who doesn't really want to have sex is a real turn-off for me because, as an intuitive person, I can feel something is off – like an energetic bucket of water is being thrown on the flames of passion and lust. It really puts the brakes on. It should be a no-brainer, really.

Around that time, I also started therapy, which helped me make sense of why sex just wasn't working with some people. Not working like it used to, that is – based on the experiences I'd had in the past. But what *would* work? What *could* work? The answer to that was a long way out of my comfort zone.

It dawned on me that the reason I felt lost and clueless had more to do with problematic learned patterns of behaviour than with my body changing because of menopause, or because of not having sex. I was a chronic people pleaser, felt responsible for fixing everyone's problems, was unable to set healthy boundaries, and avoided confrontation at all costs. My relationships were codependent and I lacked emotional maturity and healthy communication skills. I had no idea what my needs were, let alone how to communicate them. I was a perfectionist, hypervigilant ball of tension, always on high alert, always needing to 'get it right'. Which doesn't exactly create a sensual, relaxed, embodied state of being – essential for intimacy and pleasure.

Damn it. I just wanted to figure out how to have satisfying sex again, not excavate *All the Issues of My Whole Life.*

But there was no other way. I was about to find out that they were inextricably linked.

One major piece of the *Puzzle Of Me* that I discovered a few years ago was that I am neurodivergent. I don't know exactly what flavour of neurospicy I am, but being a HSP (highly sensitive person) definitely feels like a part of it.

Looking back on my life, it suddenly made sense why I was so misunderstood. Why I was bullied – because I was different. Why I took things so literally. Why I struggled so much with socialising. Why I didn't seem to get those unspoken rules of etiquette (I'm all for good manners, but etiquette can go fuck itself as far as I'm concerned).

I learned to mask very well, and I took a strange pride in that, overachiever that I am. I fawned and dissociated my way through secondary school. My bullies weren't always mean – sometimes they were perfectly friendly – but I knew they were volatile and unpredictable, and they could turn on me at any time. It often happened when others were around, but no one stood up for me or took my side. I felt unsafe and alone.

Another marker of the era I grew up in was having no autonomy. We got told, "Kiss your grandma" or "Hug your uncle" or "Go on, play with the kid next door, he likes you and he's so nice." I was never asked whether I actually *wanted* to do any of those things. No wonder I felt powerless and unimportant.

After a while of remembering my life in a new light, and beyond the grief that had been released in me, I found some glimmers of self-acceptance and self-compassion. That was a soothing balm for all the anger I had discovered. First, I was angry with other people and blamed them for my misfortune. Then I was furious with this neurotypical society because it's so unfair! Then I became *Extremely*

Fucked Off with the patriarchy, for obvious reasons. But I finally realised that those were all just reflections of how angry I was with myself. How could I allow myself to be so betrayed? Lied to? How could I let myself be so fooled?

I had to forgive myself for getting caught up in this game. It wasn't my fault. It was about survival. I learned these behaviours because I needed to be safe. It was all I had access to at the time. And it served me well, while I needed it.

But now, I saw that all these coping mechanisms had me caged. I didn't know just how much. Once you start seeing your cage, you see other people's cages, too. Or when you start to see other people's cages, you start to see your own. Some people's cages were obviously small. My own cage was of considerable size, padded with privilege, and even though the bars were hard to see, I knew I was confined nonetheless.

What does this have to do with sex? Everything. It's all entangled. Inseparable.

Gender roles keep us ALL trapped. Women are not allowed to be sexual, or assertive, or empowered. They're meant to conform and comply and just do what they're told. They need to keep themselves small – *literally* – so they don't take up too much space – *literally*. Yes, men are allowed to be sexual and assertive and empowered. But they are not allowed to be emotional, vulnerable, and talk about their feelings with others – especially other men.

As I navigated relationships after learning more about myself and my unhelpful habits, I saw just how these learned behaviours contribute to dysfunction on a bigger scale. As I dated an asexual person who wasn't out as asexual (still trying to do what society expected of them as a 'male-bodied' person), it became clear that I had some problematic beliefs and assumptions of my own.

It took me a while to find the words behind it all. It was rooted in people pleasing. The script translated as follows: *"To avoid rejection, I don't ask for anything. Instead, I give and give and give, all the time, whether you've asked me for that or not. I am putting your needs first; I am comfortable in that space because it helps me avoid my own needs. When I finally do ask for something, you can't say no. You can't refuse. That's not fair. You owe me."*

Needless to say, this was a recipe for resentment.

I see people pleasing as just an extreme, out-of-balance version of being a kind and compassionate person. There's nothing wrong with that, but blown out of proportion, it doesn't please anyone, least of all myself. In all honesty, it's manipulative, controlling and filled with entitlement.

Big ouch.

I realised that this showed up not just in my intimate relationship day-to-day, but also in sex. I hadn't noticed it before because I made sure I claimed my pleasure and orgasms. But in queer relationships, it really became obvious because some of my internalised unconscious biases were highlighted.

I realised that many 'normal' sexual experiences are often mechanical, performative, and transactional, and my experience was no different. I also learned that part of me believed that PIV (penis in vagina) sex is the 'main course' and anything else was lesser than (words like 'foreplay' don't help much in that department). Nothing wrong with enjoying PIV sex, but there's a lot more to be enjoyed besides the obvious. And having intimate experiences with folks who relate to their bodies – and genitals – differently, has been a real eye-opener.

One of my partners and I found a delightful analogy, referring to sexual preferences like dishes in a buffet. We all have our own idea of what dishes we would include in our buffet. But the problem is that we are all given a default buffet – an *Assigned Buffet At Birth* (ABAB!), if you will – and *we're not really supposed to deviate from it.* If you want to customise it or replace dishes with more unconventional ones, you're quickly seen as a sexual deviant. And if you want to take most – or all – of the dishes off the table altogether, you must be broken and your appetite needs to be fixed.

In addition, we assume that someone with a particular body (or genitals) will enjoy specific dishes because most people with that body (or genitals) do. Or, that because we enjoy a certain dish ourselves, and it is a widely enjoyed dish, of course our partner will enjoy it as well. Why do we not have these conversations? Asking someone "Do you enjoy x?" rather than just assuming they do seems so simple.

I've learned to ask my neurodivergent friends and/or partners for answers to these specific, detailed, and basic questions.

They often experience sensory overload so it's important to get into detail. Things they enjoy can be very particular and dependent on conditions. A little bite of a dish is great, but a little bit more is completely overwhelming. Or, dish X is wonderful but only if condition Y is met, and if not, it's a no-go.

Someone may have had a bad experience with a particular dish and they're now reluctant to try it again. They may be open to experimenting with it but need a lot of hand-holding.

It's important to know not just *what's* on the buffet, but *when.*

And it's just as important to know what's *not* on the buffet, *ever.*

I mean to *really* know, to understand, because it has been discussed, not just assumed.

One of the best things about this journey is that it is giving me permission to be particular, too. To own my preferences. To ask for specific things in specific ways, without feeling like I'm asking too much, or that there's something wrong with me for wanting what I want, how I want it.

So, now in my early fifties, I'm learning to cultivate intimacy *with myself*. I'm becoming a safer person – *for myself*. *To* myself. I'm no longer betraying myself by discounting my needs. I'm no longer bypassing my body's guidance. I'm more honest with myself first, and then I share that with folks who are open and willing to receive that; to receive *me*, fully. Anyone who cannot meet me in that space is not welcome.

My curiosity combined with my desire for connection, satisfaction, and pleasure, is what keeps me moving forward, even when I feel reluctant and apprehensive, would rather stay in my dysfunctional comfort zone, and avoid people altogether. That pull, that desire for more, is just that little bit stronger. That's where my focus is.

I am responding to life, experiencing it, rather than trying to figure everything out in my head first to minimise the risk of pain and rejection.

When I start to feel that niggle of resentment, I know there is more of me to be reclaimed.

I'm finally getting the hang of letting what I do, and who I am, be enough. I want to experience myself through and with others, and find and enjoy as much of me as I possibly can.

I'm still *Extremely Fucked Off* with the patriarchy. But I'm using that rage as fuel for rebellion. Even after half a century, there's still time for that. I'm only just beginning.

Entering the Bardo

BY KIMAYA CROLLA-YOUNGER

Content: cancer, disability, care recipient, masturbation, penetration

"You've got a bright future ahead," said Olga, the owner of the care agency. She was the third of a handful of folks from social services to show up in my living room, after I'd been unceremoniously dumped in an inaccessible flat, in Tottenham, by an ambulance the day before.

I smiled.

I was fucked and certainly not in any way I wanted to be. Olga pushed her blonde hair behind her ear, finally looking up and letting go of the bundle of papers she'd been gripping tightly for the last ten minutes. I'd just said this to her:

"I will fully recover... in about four years."

I'd been assigned nine hours of care support each week, which felt bewildering. The questions from a tight place in her washed over me, no substance to land, and I found my response monosyllabic. This was how this blonde, fit, clenched yet stylish woman had ended up perched on the end of my bed. She crinkled her eyes at the 'four years' bit.

In spite of being royally fucked, I was also in a state of awe and wonder, a euphoria, which bubbled up from my pelvis and as it grazed my throat, I stretched my neck up. I am alive! And this new environment felt as delicious as it gets, after more than four months in hospital without a single moment to myself; a space to really sink into! This prospect generated another smile on my face.

Olga, by this time, was crossing and uncrossing her legs like Kenny Everett and hadn't noticed my smile. I was none the wiser after our meeting, a state I'd come to expect after similar encounters with Camden services. My life seemed to have an impetus I wasn't in control of.

The next morning my phone pinged at 7 o'clock: *Good morning, Kimaya, Tyrone will be arriving at 10 a.m.*

And so, this new life began.

In the hours between the SMS and his arrival, I had no place of familiar resource to draw from. "If we never had visitors, we'd never clean" but my body uncompromisingly reminded me that I wouldn't be able to do the pre-clean clean. This realisation dropped me into a pit of shame, a gripping fist in my stomach. I was so overwhelmed by the task of getting myself ready to meet a total stranger that I somehow had to immediately let 'care' for me.

Tap, tap on the window and my fate was sealed, I had to let him in. The level of difficulty encountered just to answer the front door was bewildering and I kind of lurched out into the hallway, crashing the wheelchair and crushing my hands against the tatty, peeling walls. One of the front casters was momentarily trapped behind the radiator. I pulled hard and smacked into the back of the front door. FFS! In the pause, I could hear Tyrone's feet shuffling about on the other side. Everything was slo-mo, apart from my beating heart. I felt my hands gripping the cold, smooth, metal of the handrims as I stared at the letterbox. I found a way to lengthen my body so I could lean up, grasp the brass doorknob, and slowly peel the door open, whilst simultaneously pumping my feet to move the chair backwards, away from the door and the hazard of being flattened by it.

Tyrone's feet were now rooted as the threshold loomed between us. We took each other in. A micro-second of absolute presence. A tall, medium-built black man, in his 30s, nervously stood before me. His hoodie made me lean forward to catch sight of his face, at the same time as a grunt of greeting vaguely dropped in my direction. And I was supposed to let this man take care of me?

So much in me was silently screaming to slam the door, slink off and hide under the duvet, but instead, I brightly greeted him, saying he would have to come forward as I was unable to cross the threshold to the outside without help.

He made a joke of this, slightly cruelly taunting my disability. WTF?! I failed to find it funny and immediately pulled him up on this. Despite this epic misattunement, something in me relaxed.

In silence, we individually made our way into my flat. It was the first time someone was with me and I struggled to move backwards, with no space to turn and barely enough to get through my flat door. Every move was exhausting.

For the next three hours, I had to let him care for me. I had absolutely no idea how I was going to ask for this help, let alone yield to it.

Once we had made it out of the hallway, my attention returned to my carer. Tyrone's feet were back in action, pacing a circle on the dull, grey carpet in front of me, his eyes darting around, looking everywhere, apart from at me. An excruciating intimacy... the roles of carer and caree dictating something beyond the reality of what either of us was currently capable of emotionally. I frantically looked around the chaos of my space, searching for a task to assign him.

"Err, you can hang up my clothes in the wardrobe…", I gestured with a foot towards some bulging bin bags and he moved into, well, I wouldn't exactly use the word 'action', but the almost overwhelming pressure I felt to 'use him for care' temporarily abated and I found a sliver of resource to take a breath and consider my next instruction.

I found myself, both for lack of space and ability to appear nuanced in my movement, watching him and this act seemed to have a crippling effect on him, so I wheeled into the kitchen area, the half wall between us now giving a touch of energetic respite from the intensity. I was just beginning to discover the afternoon light pouring through the kitchen window when I heard a gasp and a rustle.

"What's going on?" I asked.

A selection of coloured frilly lingerie was secreted along the carpet by Tyrone's feet.

His whole demeanour had changed. "I. Can't. Do. That," he stammered, fixedly pointing at the aforementioned lingerie, a big grin spread across his face.

"Isn't handling sexy lingerie part of your job description?"

"It's the first time this has happened…" his voice trailed off, eyes still glued to my lacy knickers. I was looking at them too. I'd only met Tyrone 30 minutes ago and he'd already seen my knickers. It was like they were radioactive. "There's. No. Way. I. Can. Touch. Those," he said, still grinning. So, on the floor they remained, silently taunting him.

I still had two and a half hours to fill. My eyes nervously scanned to where he was standing in front of the fireplace. I had an idea. My fireplace was filled in with a crude swathe of plaster. Such lack of care typical in a rental, it contrasted the refined Italian grey marble surround – a rare and perhaps original piece from when the house was constructed.

During my months in hospital, I drew inspiration from a line at the end of my daily morning meditation; the words were so inspiring that I'd printed them out LARGE, on ten sheets of A4 paper, the black letters filling the pages. I gave Tyrone a pack of sticky putty and the sheets. Tyrone blinked and looked mystified. "You want me to stick the sheets in the fireplace?"

"Yup." I grabbed a pad near my feet and wrote out the complete sentence: *The Systems of My Body Are Drawing From A New Light.*

I got a sense that he thought I might be winding him up and this made him initially uncertain, feet again pacing, glancing to me for almost constant reassurance for the first few sheets, but after that, he gave it his all. With his energy and attention now channelled, I could begin to return to mine. Staying in the room with him this time, and with his back to me, I could take him in. Tyrone had peeled off his hoodie to reveal a short-sleeved Adidas T. His guns poked out from the sleeves. He had an old tattoo and I enjoyed trying to figure out what it was. A whole hour went by. Apart from friends, all the men I'd seen these past few months were doctors or nurses wanting to annoyingly tinker with my body. This, (how to call it?) *togetherness*, was something new. It was too early to say, but perhaps it was something I could enjoy. My reassurance to him that he'd done a good job seemed like a drink he was thirsty for.

It was three days since I'd been dumped into this studio flat in Tottenham; hey, I'd never even been to Tottenham before this. Tyrone was born and raised here, with Jamaican roots. Not only had I not been outside since I arrived, I wasn't physically able to do so by myself, due to the inaccessibility of the environment. I had to let him help me. I'd also run out of food. I couldn't even order anything online as it was currently an impossibility to make the exchange at the front door. I was vulnerable and frightened in waves.

Up to this point, I'd had little experience of being in a wheelchair – only around hospital corridors and grounds, and when friends took me to local coffee shops and restaurants. This meant I was effectively putting myself in the hands of someone I'd met 90 minutes ago. My physical vulnerability *heightened everything* and I opened myself to feel it all.

It was the only true power I had – not to suppress or repress what needed to be said, felt or rawly acknowledged.

After a lifetime of fierce independence, I was now being asked to acquiesce and let this man guide me around the back streets of Tottenham. Just to get outside my flat and safely onto the pavement was literally terrifying to me. A steep concrete slope had to be navigated and as Tyrone started to wheel/push me, I could feel my body slipping out of the chair. Maximum intensity was mixed with poignant vulnerability, my instincts were intact and I screamed out as a way of modulating the terror of the reality of having to go through this if I wanted to go out.

The amount of adrenaline surging through my system just from the challenge of getting over the few metres from the front door to the pavement was insane! I survived it that first day of being out; how strange it was to be pushed around by an entity I couldn't see. My soul shrunk as I saw my neighbours' broken windows, overgrown weeds, discarded toys, armchairs and fridges. No love, no beauty. Poverty incarnate.

It took a few trips to discover the shortest route to the main road and for us to find a way of synchronising my vision of where I felt was safe and most comfortable to be wheeled and where he actually took me. Tyrone had to translate my cries of 'No!', 'Eek', 'Argh', 'Stop'.

Two weeks passed. At home, I was mainly alone and mainly in the wheelchair, and because I was in it, I didn't *see* it. It became a part of me. The slowness of what was possible with my movement, and how I approached each practicality, had to be intentional. I was often unsure how to approach even the tiniest task without either falling or hurting myself. This permanent snail's pace of life amplified my perception, nothing escaped its magnifying quality. My flat became my entire world and I had never felt so alive! When Tyrone entered my space each day, he was entering so much more than he or I realised. The space in my flat became an extension of my body and just this simple, ordinary act, of this man stepping into the totality of my environment, felt indescribably intimate and activating.

Anything he touched, anything he moved, had great impact on me. If he put the lid back on something that I'd asked him not to, I would have to wait for his return to take the lid back off. Him moving an item, any item, often meant that it was now either out of reach or I didn't have the dexterity required to open or prepare something, and it would typically mean not being able to brush my teeth or eat that night. When this was the case, an intensity would rise in me like a steam train. I would become enraged, then humiliated, followed by sobbing, until eventually I was wiped clean from the tears and at peace. My life was becoming an unending torrent of challenge and frustration that was never going away. I had to find new ways to meet it before it would crush me.

Tyrone told me a little about Tottenham and his life there. I was conscious of my own comments about the place, how jarring, unfamiliar and, well, scary really, I found it, particularly the large groups of brooding men, dressed in tatty sportswear and gathered in the streets, that I had to pass by. As a strong, independent woman with plenty of street smarts and nearly six feet tall, it was a very different sensation in a wheelchair, where I was reduced in stature to the height I was when I was a child.

After the first month, there was something of a flavour of getting ready for a date. Each morning in bed, my body needed my undivided attention to meet the places of tightness and numbness and breathe life into them. I had to wait until I was ready. My mind would wander to a part of me that felt like a teenager, and would suggest things like 'What about that black dress?' or 'Those earrings with the feathers would look nice with my red leather jacket'.

Each day, when the timing was right, movement would slowly begin and I would reach out and grab one of the metal handrails that were either side of my mattress for support. My bed had a quality of quicksand – great for when I wanted to be in it, totally crap for trying to get out of it – and this quality, together with my immobility and the force of gravity, made it extraordinarily difficult to do any kind of moving across it. Just to manoeuvre myself to the edge was a Herculean task; my normally elegant way of organising myself was long gone, I had to take any way I could, which currently involved hauling myself, like a big piece of meat across the sucky fucking surface of the mattress, accompanied by me shouting "For fuck's sake!" into space, or hysterically laughing. More often than not, a stylish combo of the two. When I finally got to the edge of the bed, I had to take some minutes to recover, before gently, tenderly and somewhat triumphantly decanting myself into the wheelchair. Now, where did I put that little black dress...

* * *

It was our third week and we were in a kind of sweet rhythm. I would greet Tyrone at the door and the first part of the session would involve him taking me out for shopping or lunch. We'd then return home and the contrast of being in the outside world, where we'd had such enlivening exchanges, became compressed once we were in the small space of my flat. There was a tangible buoyancy in the space between us which I can't say I've experienced with anyone else to this day. The buoyancy felt like an invitation, unspoken, to a place in me that said, "Yes, you can have me, all you have to do is reach out and take it." It was activated when we were within brushing distance of each other. Proximity as a form of touch. I'm sure he started wearing more tight-fitting clothes, or perhaps the nuance of my attention was becoming amplified by the chemistry between us. In time, I think he truly felt useful and appreciated by me, qualities that seemed heartbreakingly absent from his life away from me.

As time went by, our conversations, as Tyrone wheeled me around the streets of Tottenham, became more... daring. The normal rules of body language no longer applied. We were connected, albeit by the chassis of my metal chaperone and with Tyrone pushing from behind. I did my own pushing – of emotional boundaries. With my body firmly held in metal, facing forward, the lack of visual contact elicited a naughty, emotional bravery in me. Asking him more and more intimate questions felt edgy and exciting. I couldn't see his face when I asked, "How was your sexual energy affected by not eating meat?" These inquiries dropped like little grenades from my lips, launching into space. They were followed by a pregnant pause (that was so loooooong) before he responded, and I could only micro-squirm around in my seat without him seeing me. What a thrill. This power that I had. He was there to serve me and I played with, had fun with, and pushed it. Of course, I can't speak for Tyrone, but he seemed like a willing kind of playmate.

The transforming fires of my daylight hours, of being propelled into the most extreme states imaginable, emotionally and physically, of being viscerally exposed, left me facing waves of intensity that crashed into overwhelm. Such accumulation needed to go somewhere; it needed a shepherding into the depths of me. It was compost for Eros.

The raw energy of life, and living on the edge of instincts, permeated the environment and those around me in our little flats (that were really rooms in the same house, separated by flimsy front doors and creaking, leaking ceilings and floors). The parts of us that came to the fore in daylight hours were not the same parts that revealed themselves at the fall of darkness. One particular night, a twisted voice from a Jamaican guy in the flat above me boomed out of the ceiling, "I'm gonna fuck you up, *pussyclaat.*" I thought this was how his dad had probably spoken to him when he was a boy. I remembered my own nights of feeling scared at home in the dark. This night was now a new one; the unexpected threatening voice opened a chaos in my system, a familiar bone-deep, gnawing terror.

Life was changing me. I'd always had white or cream-coloured bedding but, lately, my spirit wanted black, blackness… In my hours of meditation, I held focus in the void, the blackness of consciousness. This blackness nourished the very cells of me. Lying on my side for the first time on my new black sheet, I pushed the duvet off of me, my eyes taking in the contrast of my skin against the bedding. My naked body was illuminated in the soft glow of my salt lamps, the light bestowed my skin with a kind of radiance only gifted in semi-darkness. My chest rose up and down, activated by the disembodied, menacing voice above, his words had found a way in, soaking me in a fear I couldn't escape from, and which ceilings and walls couldn't keep out.

All of me, all of me, a part of me whispered. My feet pushed out, searching for some contact in the dark, found the discarded duvet and trod it off the bed with a satisfying 'plomp' on the floor. I paused. Still, yet potent, my body was shaped like a crescent moon in the night sky, the white ceiling above a bright voyeur to an unfolding below. My breath, in this moment, became the only sense that mattered; it tried to grow larger but it was tight in the cage of my chest and had given up long ago trying to take the space it needed to meet the terror – it didn't even know if more space *could* be possible. *Everything is here for me.* Something inside me, invisible, seemed to know what to do, what was wanting to be known, what would bring, what? Pleasure? I didn't, couldn't, have an agenda other than life moving through me. My breath, my belly, became the auditorium of possibility, of totality. Waiting, waiting. Then...

I felt shackles releasing.

...and my senses returned. Acute awareness of this feminine body, everything was curved, ripe, flowering in the dark, for me only. I let out a giggle, glanced up and the ceiling encouraged me to try something new. The crescent of me lying on my left side, this part of me engulfed in my bed, everything supported. I *knew* that I wanted to reach *everywhere* and my body responded by curling in a little more. My left hand started to respond to a longing in my breasts to be held. This hand, animated by love itself, approached my right breast with a tenderness and reverence I had never before known. Every place of my palm undulating, pressing, letting me know by the quality of touch this breast belonged to me, how loved it was, not settling to rest until it had explored and caressed every (neglected?) place; places I don't think I'd ever touched, apart from in a perfunctory or coarsely sexual way. The touching didn't stop until I had fully got the message of how cherished my right breast was, how unique and a part of me. A tear rolled down my cheek.

Something was birthed in me that night. A couple of hours went by. My breath continued to hold me. A sheath around my skin. A flame in my solar plexus, my breath knew what to do, it held its attention; a place in me began a lovemaking. My open mouth next to my heightened skin, with the curve of my shoulder almost cradling my cheek. I exhaled, breath lightly catching at the back of my throat, an audible sound of bliss, satisfaction, that enveloped my ears, a sound of safety that opened a place in me. The flame grew larger, covering the entirety of my torso. Deeply guided, all doing was given over to existence herself. An initiation into something primordial, encoded. So unexpected, I'm not sure what to call it: a visitation? Not fantasy. I became aware of a masculine presence behind me, spooning me, a black masculine presence, that I was communing with, via the skin, drinking in this presence. Something frozen was thawing, bringing parts of me into the present moment for the first time, an orchestration that my body was curating. After allowing myself to be brutalised by so much, now, in this bed, in this darkness, it all turned to beauty.

* * *

The sun was streaming through my window, onto my face and body, basking in the afterglow of contact and interacting with this man, my carer. The wheelchair, stifling nuanced movement, acted as a vice, squeezing, pushing the life that was surging through me, *deeper into me.* The metal made me face forward, legs clamped shut. Hips locked. Micro-movements of eros, barely discernible to an outside eye, became a tidal wave of *YES!* My next breath entered my feet, rippling up my legs, gathering momentum, flooding the ripe space between my hips; I suddenly felt off balance, out of control, and had to open my eyes.

I had a thrilling thought as I reached for my smartphone, I recalled a visual scene, some porn that I could reliably trust to get me off. Urgency building, hands trembling as I keyed in the website name. Up popped: *You are not allowed to view this, you naughty girl!* Well, it didn't exactly say that but the blocked adult content screen flashing in my face sure made me feel that way. Damn it. I dived into the settings, seeking permission. "Give it to me, you tyrant!" Nope. Argh. One more try and another cock-blocking message.

Okay, I got it, perhaps this habit was no longer the way. I wasn't put off or deflated. There was an urgency, yet underneath that, I was curious if I could find a way to be with this surging and follow it, hold it instead of throwing it off.

It was the first time in many months that my body and environment were in sync. The slowness of my current life, the smallness of it even, made this erotic visitation one that I had time to explore. Could I hold the complexity of what was here in this moment, a kind of sensitive chaos?

I was drawn to getting my body in a certain shape, one where I could be penetrated. Climbing onto my bed, on all fours, body guiding me, a doubtful part of me thought my hotness would melt away without immediate direct attention. I slowly turned onto my back, releasing the great effort involved in moving, sighing from this sweet surrender as gravity took over and I absorbed the softness of my quilt. Coupled with a new intensity of being held by the bed, this allowed the woman in me to come further forward.

The position of my body felt important: the angle of my head had to allow a flow in my throat; and something under my hips for a certain tilt. A pillow at the back of my heart created a soft arc that gave the Cosmos access to my nipples. I was ready. A stillness entered me. I wanted to be penetrated by the masculine... a blackness I wanted to be claimed by. No sooner had this thought arisen, and I could feel... He. Was. In. Me. Deep in the petals of my pussy. My focus, my complete attention went to her...

My pussy was filling up with it all. The pace quickened. I felt an immense desire to open her more; a flash went through my mind of a sheela na gig opening her pussy to life itself. In the urgency, my body's habituated self-pleasure pattern became dominant and I managed to scramble across and to the edge of the bed, contracting the muscles in my legs, hips pushing, pushing the sexual energy into my sex. I pinched my nipples hard. Life had brought me so much since I'd last self-pleasured – massive immobility, a cancer diagnosis – I honestly wondered if it was still possible to climax. It was! It was utterly glorious, rippling through places of numbness that my body was slowly beginning to feel again after the cancer.

***

Eros arose in me outside of any 'conventional' container, I learnt to hold the delicious charge, savour it, trust it, follow it, *go* to where I felt most drawn. Particularly when it came to my mobility. Eros was an antidote to rigidity.

* * *

One sweet morning, I was following a recording of a somatic practice that engages with the body as a fluid system; the title of the class, *The Liquid Heart*, touched into a place of ecstasy that continued to open as I was guided by the voice from my laptop. Remaining true to a first-order somatic deep experience, I experienced a belonging to the wild sensation of 'right now'. After a time on my side, I was drawn to being on all fours. With my breasts free to roam the soft surface underneath, my nipples lightly grazed the material. My palms pressed firmly into the surface, gliding myself forward. Eros was suddenly there, ignited by the nipple graze, and I dived in, giggling – my breasts wanted me to know they belonged to the liquid heart, despite them not being explicitly invited by the laptop voice.

* * *

"Sit up straight, keep your back erect, relax your body."

The American voice I'd heard hundreds of times rang out warmly in my living room that morning. Through years of almost daily meditation, I'd become really practised at inner body attunement, particularly with staying with numbness or compression in the heart and yoni. I'd experienced all kinds of variations of where to put my attention and what to notice once I got there.

I'd carved out a dedicated space and to get there it involved transferring from the wheelchair, relying on my ever-increasing upper body strength and dropping myself into a chocolate brown, massive-bear-of-a-thing, leather armchair, retro style with high sides and stocky wooden feet.

This was a place I felt completely held... I felt support in all the right places: my entire thighs, all the way to the back of the knees, enabling just the right holding for my bottom and pelvis to spread out, and most importantly, my yoni to come back online. This was in stark contrast to the way my hips were clamped shut by the metal skirt of the wheelchair for most of my day. The entirety of my mid-torso was held, drawing a line up my spine as my body pressed deeply into the cool leather at the space surrounding the back of my heart and across my shoulder blades. My feet and lower legs could explore at their leisure.

This was a quality of support that invited complete surrender. I let out a massive sigh from the immediate pleasure of every muscle in my upper body releasing the intense gripping from holding the extra weight, always laced with a fear that I might fall. The air powered through my lungs like fine rivulets of volcanic lava, and spilled into my breasts – which playfully nudged the soft warm skin on the inside of my upper arms. My fingers straddled the width of the wide armrests, pressing down strongly, dragging the bare skin of my wrists and palms slowly forward along the sweeping, feminine curve of the design. I ate up the strong sensation of the cool leather and rough, rugged stitching where the edges of the leather met. I didn't press play until my body wanted it.

The soundtrack immediately felt really good. Slow, sensual beats, a gorgeous, languorous rhythm. Cicadas opened up delicious layers of warmth and relaxation, like thick, golden waves cascading through every place of me that had been previously isolated from this flow. Instantly evocative, the mood got into the roots of me. Everything felt instinctual.

"Love yourself enough to do this…"

I brought my focus to a pulsation in the tissues of my yoni, each pulse sweetly probing a place that had lived darkly in her. Where she had believed certain dark things. And allowed certain things to happen, in order to not be alone. I stayed here for a while, glimmering in a kind of fugitive light, turning up the volume of my attention, my body leading by pressing into the leather behind me at the base of my neck, inviting my head/mind to drop back in a gesture of submission and respect to what was beginning to unfold. Caring not to add so much as a gram of force or expectation…

After *endless* holding, I felt a bondage releasing in the dark of Her. My thighs, witnessing, became two white pillars of protection, guiding His frequency through all crevices and corners where the mystery continued to dwell; electric waves of wetness, gathering power. I held my breath and felt a coming and going of excitement on the shores of my sex. Lightly clenching the top of my thighs and sustaining the contraction, at the same time as pursing my lips and slowly breathing out as if to breathe on my lover's chest, I felt a fine vibration throughout my entire body. The vibration began to deepen, and as I stayed with the contraction, everything turned into a pulsating. Then a tsunami of *let it go* took over, plunged into everything, everywhere, all at once, and I became aware of a streaming, an internal flowing. I was it. A filling up of the inner and outer lips of my pussy, surging through all the places in her. Pure presence as the fuel, amplifying the interior. This liquid environment, high up in the internal petals was He, his etheric lingam. Still. Not moving. Penetrating. Felt fully through the flesh. Undivided. The deep, felt sense of reciprocity in my pussy made me call out "Yeah baby!"

This streaming of lovemaking, utterly audacious, simply natural. I lay basking in a kind of blissed-out stupor for a long time afterwards.

* * *

I told some friends I was in love with my carer, of course, the whole world was going on in this tiny statement! Two complex humans suddenly finding themselves spending big chunks of time together, with a pretty firm structure of what that time was for. We'd never have met each other in any other circumstance. I found this pretty wild to contemplate. There was a delicious friction between us, that ultimately, for me, broke the container. The narrative of my first days out of hospital, and the beginning of my experience of social services and care, frame well the beginning stages of huge change in my lived experience. I am grateful for my time with my carer Tyrone; the touches of masculine frequency, his openness, his intact soul, our attraction and how we vibed and played with it, with just enough goodness to echo through me. This goodness will forever remain in my heart. Our meetings, I felt, were a medicine to the challenges of our lives. I had tastes of what was going on for him. Trauma weaved in and out of both of our daily lives.

* * *

When I contemplate the essential qualities of my solo erotic explorations, what was opened in me, the bone-deep satisfaction, I can say it by far eclipses many past *in-the-flesh* sexual experiences, and I move ever forward in a refined discernment of opening to meet the life *that's here*, and allowing the world to support me in the endeavour to meet it.

After around two years of being out of balance with rapidly declining health, leading to two diagnoses and a long hospital stay, moving to Tottenham marked a slow trajectory towards thriving. I can see, looking back, this time was an alchemy of so much; building on my instinctual ways of thinking and being, involving digging even deeper than I previously had – fortunately, a natural fascination for me, that I heavily invest in to this day. What really made a difference was finding ways to acknowledge, clear and allow a slow-motion kind of release of deeply held soul shock and resulting beliefs at a cellular level, and clearing the impact to my self-esteem (all of this is ongoing, for life). Opening to the nourishment of the land beneath me, the sanctuary of my home, my daily practices, *this* created a *Field of Eros*, that imbued my waking moments. My memory of this time has etched in me a golden imprint, a life buoy that I return to as a resource to draw from as I move with new challenges in ever more creative ways.

Becoming Me:
a Story of Four Women
and Two Men

BY EVE RAY

Content: *gender transition, transphobia, kink and BDSM, oral sex,
friendship and support*

Author's note:

*The story below is one I knew I wanted to tell when Anna
approached me about contributing to this anthology.
Emma's story is not quite mine, although parts of it are fic-
tionalised versions of events that have happened in my life.*

*I wanted to look at the question of what makes a
trans woman a woman. Social media is full of vitriolic
exchanges between those who claim that transwomen are
women and those who deny this. But the question needs
to be asked, and consideration of the answer needs to go
beyond slogans. My personal experience is that it is the
relationships we have and the friendships we form, that,
in large measure, make us who we are. Thus, this story is
about relationships and friendships. I want to stress the
friendships because, although I am a writer of erotica and
a sex blogger, platonic friendships with women have been
as important to me as sexual and kink relationships. My*

closest friends are women; I am in at least three girl gangs. I am accepted as a woman by women who can relate to me and want me as a friend. I only ever hoped for acceptance. What I have received is friendship and love. These friendships have changed me.

I have also found that gender transition is not something that sits in isolation from other changes in a person's life but interacts with them. Without my transition, I do not think I would be bisexual (with a primary attraction to men) and a dominant in my BDSM life. I have discovered the delights of giving a man oral, I have experienced the intoxicating thrill of having a submissive man restrained and at my mercy, then felt humbled at the trust placed in me. This, too, has changed me.

Talking of sexual encounters, as you read the story you will see that Emma – a trans woman – refers to her penis. Please remember that her genitals – and her choices about the words she uses for them – do not take anything away from her being a woman.

I sometimes compare transition to learning a language. Living as a woman and not having friendships with women would be a bit like learning French and never going to France, never using the language to engage with others, or buying an artisan cheese and a bottle of Vin de Pays at a farmers' market. I do this at a local market near where I live. And now that I'm a woman, I have some really lovely friends to share them with.

* * *

I'm Emma, a 53-year-old trans woman who has been out and proud for ten years. A trans woman I said, not a bloke in a frock (though I love frocks!). What makes me a woman? People do. People make me who I am. Here is the story of my journey, told through encounters with six people who have made it all worthwhile.

Kevin

Kevin stared hard at the woman who had just walked into the pub. He grimaced. "The state of that!" he said, almost spitting his beer out. "You can see from here it's not a real woman!"

"What is she then?" I asked.

"It's a tranny."

"A what?"

"You know, a transvestite. Blokes who like wearing dresses. Perverts! Just look at those hands, like fucking shovels and it thinks it's a woman."

"Yeah, I suppose."

The woman stood at the bar, looking around nervously. Was she waiting for someone? Or did she just want people to think that to make herself feel less vulnerable? I thought she looked quite pretty. A bit unusual, certainly, but was she so obviously a bloke?

While Kevin went to the Gents, I went to get the next round in. I stood next to her at the bar, and we made eye contact. She smiled. "Hello," she said. Her voice sounded like she'd intentionally raised its pitch, but it was warm and friendly.

"Hi," I replied, desperately thinking of what to say next.

"You are talking to me then, lovely?"

"Yeah, why not?"

"I don't think your friend approves of me." She gestured towards the door of the Gents.

I looked down and shuffled my feet. I really did have nothing to say to that.

"Well, you know what?" she continued.

"What?"

"I couldn't give a shit what he thinks. I know what I'm worth and no one is going to laugh at me because my hands are a bit bigger than the average girl's, or my voice a bit deeper."

I said nothing.

"Do you understand me? Well, do you?"

"I do."

I saw Kevin making his way back to our table. I caught the barman's eye and ordered two more pints. As I moved away from the bar with our drinks, the woman smiled and said quite audibly, "Lovely chatting to you!"

Kevin glared.

Steph

My mind was now made up and the next time I set foot inside a pub I was wearing a leopard-print dress and low heels.

With my best friend and former lover – Stephanie – I had checked into a budget hotel room on the edge of the city's Gay Village. Once in the room, we opened a bottle of wine and she helped me get ready. She dressed me and did my make-up, with a skill and touch I couldn't imagine ever mastering. As we left the hotel, she put her arm around me in reassurance. I walked clumsily, still unused to heels. I worried that everyone was staring at me, and making the kind of contemptuous comments I'd heard Kevin make the previous week.

Thankfully, we soon reached the gay bar. It would be packed on Friday nights but was nearly empty so early on this cold Thursday evening. We each ordered a G&T and sat down at one of the many free tables.

"You haven't got much to say tonight, Emma?" Steph

took a sip of her drink and waited for me to reply.

I tried to pitch my voice at what I thought was a feminine level. "I don't. I just keep thinking about things."

"Like what?"

"Like how I wanted to do this so much and how I'm so nervous about it all," I admitted.

"Don't worry about that. It will soon pass. You're being you, aren't you? Wait till you get more comfortable in your own skin. And when you do, there will be no stopping you. Just wait and see."

"Maybe a cigarette will help," I said and headed outside to the beer garden.

I took out a cigarette and fumbled in my bag for my lighter. I had forgotten it. Damn! I was going to have to approach the young man smoking on his own at the next table. "Have you got a light?" I asked. He held out a lighter. "You could light a cigarette for a lady," I said, suddenly more confident.

"I'm sorry," he said and stood up as he offered the flame to the tip of my cigarette.

I drew the smoke deep into my lungs and sat down. I felt better already.

"I admire you doing this," he said, "you know, just getting on and being yourself like that. It takes balls." He laughed at the sudden realisation of what he had said. "Sorry, but you know what I mean."

I smiled. "Yes, I do."

"I came out as gay when I was sixteen," he continued. "My parents disowned me. My dad called me a pervert and said they were both ashamed to have brought someone like me into the world." He was thoughtful for a moment. "So, I went and told my nan. She was totally cool about it. She was the older generation but more accepting. Funny how things go. But I am happy for you that you can do this. I really hope it all goes well for you."

We finished our cigarettes and I went back to Steph.

After the bar, we headed to a nearby restaurant. The waiter addressed me as Madam, which shocked me to the extent that I didn't realise he meant me. I looked hurriedly around to see who he might be talking to.

Meal eaten, I walked with Steph to the train station. "Are you sure you're alright going back to the hotel on your own?" she checked.

"I'll be fine. I'm feeling okay now. I don't feel like everyone is staring at me any more." We hugged, a hug of friends, not lovers, with kisses on cheeks, and I returned to the hotel alone, confident and happy. I now understood the confidence of the woman I had met in the pub the previous week. And I'd realised something else: no one was giving me a second glance; people were mostly too busy getting on with their own lives to judge others. Those who weren't explicitly supportive of trans people were either accepting or couldn't give a damn. And this was a good thing too. There really weren't many Kevins.

Back at the hotel, I showered and put on my favourite floral print nightdress. I got into my bed and took out my vibrator and favourite porn – an old copy of German Playboy. But, this time, it didn't work for me. All I saw was women presented for the male gaze. As I looked into Magdalena's eyes on page 14, I found myself admiring her beautiful make-up and realised I didn't want to fuck her, I wanted to be her.

Jane

"Why don't you get your eyebrows threaded?" Jane asked as I looked in the mirror and adjusted my make-up.

"What's that?" I asked.

"It's a great way to make them look more defined, a bit more feminine. Yours are quite bushy..."

"Feminine?"

"Emma, you're lovely as you are, but you really could do with working on your look. It's all part of being a woman. Do you get your legs waxed?"

I glanced down at my calves hidden behind their 60 deniers. "No."

"I do, I hate having hairy legs and love it when they feel so smooth. But, you know, I do sometimes wonder why we do it: the money, and the pain and all that. But it's what we women have to do. Anyway, let's touch up your make-up. Got a powder compact?"

I did. I reached into my bag, found my compact and handed it to her. I loved the sensation as she deftly ran the little pad over my skin. I squeezed my eyes shut and smiled as she dabbed my cheeks.

"You like that?"

"It tickles!"

"Come on, let's do your lippy."

I pulled my lipstick from my bag and offered it to her.

"Try mine," Jane said and showed me a long black tube with a magenta-pink top.

"This is a good shade for you." She ran the wand over my lips. "Pucker." I did as I was told. "Brilliant. Now you look like a proper woman. See for yourself."

I looked in the mirror. Jane had done a good job. But there was more to it than that. More to it than her guileless friendliness. It was a moment of female complicity in the faux-retro toilets of a crowded Saturday night pub. It was a beautiful belonging and the realisation that Jane understood I needed help to belong.

We went back into the bar and Jane ordered us cocktails. "We've got the same," she said, "that way we get two for the price of one. This one's called *Suck It and Swallow*." She handed me the glass.

"Well, that does sound promising," I quipped.

"Doesn't it?" Jane laughed so much she snorted. "Sorry!" she said.

We sucked at the straws. The cocktail had a bubble gum taste, not at all unpleasant.

"Got a bloke yet, Emma?"

"No, I'm not sure –"

"Have you ever been with a guy?" Jane interrupted.

I focused my attention on my drink and said nothing.

"But you're a girl now, Emma, I reckon you could be quite fanciable from a bloke's perspective. Do you want me to fix you up with someone?"

I hesitated before replying, "I'm not sure I can though."

"You haven't had the op, you haven't got a fanny? Is that what you're trying to tell me?"

I nodded. Jane sucked hard at the straw, filling her mouth with the sweet pink cocktail. She blew her cheeks out and swallowed with a loud gulp. "Who needs a fanny when you've got a big sensual mouth?" She leaned across to me and, instinctively, I moved to kiss her. She pulled away. "I love you, Emma, but not that way. Let's not spoil things."

She smiled gently and ran a finger down my cheek. "What I mean is, lots of guys prefer being blown to fucking. And what girl doesn't like a mouthful of cock?"

I didn't know what to say. It wasn't that I hadn't thought about it but, as Emma, I'd never had this kind of conversation before. Let alone in such a public place.

She ran her finger over my lips.

"There's a guy I'd like you to meet. He has a thing about older women. And he'll appreciate you, I know. You're not for everyone. You're special. He will get you." She took a pad out of her bag, scribbled a name and number on the top sheet, tore it off and handed it to me. "I've got to dash. Early shift tomorrow. Give me a ring next week and we'll meet up."

She stood up, bending to kiss me on the cheek before turning quickly and leaving without a backward glance. I folded the paper and put it in my bag. I liked the idea of sucking cock and felt my own hardening at the thought. I looked down. The bulge underneath my dress was too prominent. Carefully using my bag to hide it, I went back to the Ladies. I sat down in a cubicle, in the strange orange-yellow light of a naked bulb, and played with myself. I came into a piece of toilet paper, trying hard not to gasp audibly. I was happy. I had a new friend. I had the feeling that my life was going to take another intriguing turn. And I could go back to the bar confident that everything was hidden underneath my dress again and would not give me away.

Anna

"Bite on that!"

Mistress Anna held a crop in front of my mouth as I lay strapped tightly to the spanking bench. She had walked around me, slowly, making her heeled boots reverberate on the polished wooden floor of the fetish club dungeon. It was after midnight, but I wasn't tired. I was high on a mix of dread and anticipation. Mistress was going to surprise me at some point in our scene. She always did.

"Kiss the crop and bite on it! I've told you once already." She squatted in front of me and grabbed a handful of my hair to pull my head up so that I looked straight into her face. "You do as you're told or you get hurt. Do I make myself clear?"

"Yes, Mistress." I took the crop between my teeth and bit hard, determined not to drop it.

The first blow of the paddle landed. I winced and breathed out heavily but kept the crop clamped between my jaws.

"Count the strokes and thank me."

"One, thank you, Mistress," I mumbled.

"Speak clearly!"

"Sorry, Mistress," my tongue managed to push the words out from behind my teeth.

Another stroke landed – harder and even more delicious than the first.

"Two, thank you, Mistress."

She walked around to look at me again. She was grinning mischievously. "Is it difficult to speak clearly with a crop in your mouth?"

"Yes, Mistress."

She laughed. "I so enjoy putting you in a predicament. Now you have a choice. You can either continue to mumble and have ten extra strokes for not speaking clearly, or you can drop the crop and have five strokes with that."

I opened my mouth and the crop fell to the floor.

"The second, please, Mistress."

She laughed. "You are so transparent. You'd make a rubbish poker player!"

Good to her word, Anna delivered five clean strokes with the crop. Then she untied me, helped me to sit up, and wrapped a blanket around me. She hugged me and whispered, "Well done. Did you enjoy that?" I nodded then slid down onto my knees and kissed her long leather gloves as a sign of my appreciation. "I've got a guy to deal with now.

I want you to stay and help me Domme him. Will you?"

I was so surprised by her invitation that I agreed without thinking.

When David was tied down, and Anna had warmed him up with a hand spanking, she handed me a paddle. I walked up to my secured victim, gave his red buttocks a gentle squeeze, and showed him the paddle.

"Kiss it!" I commanded, my voice clear and loud.

"Yes, Mistress," he said quietly and placed a gentle, reverential kiss on the varnished wood.

"Why does the paddle have holes in it?" I asked him.

"I don't know, Mistress."

"The holes let it move faster through the air. That way I can hurt you more."

He said nothing and I could see him bracing his restrained body, steeling himself for the pain to come.

"You will count the strokes," I told him as I got into position. I dragged my fingernails over his eager buttocks. "Ready?" I weighed the paddle once more in my hand, getting a feel for it, and then brought it swiftly down on the sweet spot of his cheek. He gasped and thanked me. This felt good.

Once we had finished our scene with David, Anna said, "You looked like you were enjoying that."

"Yes, Mistress," I answered smiling, "I did."

She was gorgeous in her PVC outfit and her boots reflected a shaft of light from a spotlight in the otherwise dim dungeon. I longed to kiss them and moved to kneel before her but she anticipated my movement and stopped me.

"Wait," she said. "I don't want you to submit to me any more." She saw my disappointment and quickly continued, "Instead, I want you to be my sister in domination! I want to show you how beautiful femdom is from this side." She kissed me on the lips. Her mouth was closed but I knew that this was a gesture of intimacy. I was going to be inducted into a new sisterhood. She was allowing me to get closer to her than I ever could as a sub. Once again, I felt a deep sense of new belonging.

Paula

"Are you a Domme now then?" asked Paula, her eyes lighting up at the thought.

"I suppose I am."

"Do you think you could dominate me?"

There was a mischievous challenge in her expression. I knew I wanted to meet this challenge, not with a man in a dungeon – which, up until now, was the only place I'd played as a dominant – but here, with Paula, in the garden of this gay bar on a warm August evening.

It was still early and we were alone in the garden. I drew on my cigarette and looked at her, reflexively closing my left eye to focus on her more intently. She suddenly looked uncomfortable but, as I blew the smoke out, she leaned forward to breathe it in.

"You should be kneeling," I told her. She dropped down onto the gravel without demur and knelt, head bowed. "Does it hurt as the stones dig into your knees?"

"Yes, Mistress."

"Good." I stood over her and drew on my cigarette again. I saw her glance up, hungrily eyeing the tip. "Do you want this?" I asked, flicking a little of the ash into my palm.

"Yes, Mistress," she said. Then, "I want you to use me as your ashtray. Please, Mistress."

"Open your mouth wide." I watched as she quickly complied. I took another draw, then flicked the gathered ash from the end of my cigarette onto her tongue. "Now swallow it." As she did so, I took a final drag on the cigarette. "Good girl. Now, get up."

I was aware that other people were beginning to enter the garden and led Paula to an empty bench. Just as we sat down, a bulky man joined us, sitting next to me with his legs wide apart, and forcing Paula and me closer together. I put my arm around her and gave her an exploratory squeeze. She didn't resist and rested her head on my shoulder. I pushed back against the man who was taking up too much space. He grunted his annoyance and drew his knees together, at least for a few seconds before opening his legs again, forcing me to slide across the bench so that Paula nearly fell off the end.

"Bloody manspreader," I whispered in her ear, and we laughed conspiratorially.

I bought us another round of cocktails and we sat and drank, suddenly not saying much. I put my arm around her again and felt the warmth of her body. I wanted to kiss her, or at least ask her if I could.

"I need the loo," Paula said.

"I'll wait for you here," I replied.

"Or you could come with me," Paula suggested with a brazen wink.

She followed as I led the way to the Ladies. I entered one of the two cubicles, turned to lock the door and saw that she had come in with me. She locked the door and leaned against it, taking off her top and bra.

"I want you," she said quietly.

I kissed her breasts and felt her nipples harden as my tongue went to work. She fumbled with her belt for a moment and then pulled down her jeans and panties. This time, I knelt, and I lapped greedily at her gloriously hairy cunt.

"Will you fuck me?" she asked.

"Sorry darling. I don't want to do that with women. Not any more."

"Stand up then."

As I stood, she lifted the hem of my dress and pulled it partly over my head so that I couldn't see her. I felt her pull down my panties as she dropped to her knees. Her tongue flicked the tip of my penis and I felt it harden. She worked her mouth over me, sucking and licking, and bringing me to a quick orgasm. She rearranged my dress as she stood up but my panties, now wet from the floor, remained around my ankles. The moist tip of my cock brushed against the cotton of my dress and a stain formed, small as a penny at first but expanding to a highly visible mark. Paula giggled.

"Consider yourself lucky," she said. "Not every girl here tonight is going to have one of those!"

I leaned in and kissed her, tasting myself on her lips. "I am blessed."

"You sure are, Lady," she said and giggled again.

John

Male bodies repelled me. I had bad memories of gym and games at my all-boys school, of close contact with sweaty, smelly adolescent bodies, the humiliations in the showers, and boys laughing at the size of each other's cocks. The realisation that mature male bodies were different, felt different, smelt different, and that the hair on those bodies could be a source of sensual delight, was slow to come. I had been ashamed of my own male body and avoided sport, exercise, and communal changing rooms. I missed out.

I missed out because, as I began to transition, I knew very quickly that I was attracted to men. It was a sudden realisation, finding myself thinking about cocks, conjuring up a fantasy of being post-operation and in bed with a muscular, hairy man who thrust his magnificent cock into my tight surgical cunt.

There was a guy who turned my head as I walked down the Tottenham Court Road one sunny afternoon. Two days unshaven (which looked like carefully curated stubble) and a firm butt poured into skinny jeans. He was hot!

I told Steph.

"That's good, isn't it?" she said. "I mean, I'm not into you that way any more. If you're not into me, that's a good thing too, isn't it?"

"I guess I could still be into women but, yeah, I need to sleep with a guy," I concluded.

Jane had tried to set me up with a guy but it hadn't come to anything. Then I met John. He was an older man who had divorced in his fifties and remained single. I guess he wanted companionship and cuddles as much as sex. He was quite shy, and lacking confidence in some ways, but we liked each other. And most importantly, he wanted to get close to me – close to the body which, even after months of hormones, I still saw as something to be ashamed of.

I wasn't ready to invite him to my home or to go to his, so we went to a swingers' club and made out in a bedroom. I took the lead. Pressed him close, kissed him, forcing my tongue into his mouth. He responded and I felt his hands against the back of my head as he pulled me in and quelled my soft tongue with his own. He pushed me gently onto the bed, got on top, kissed me, nibbled my ears, and kneaded my emerging breasts with big hands. I reached out, grabbed a handful of the hairs on his chest, and tugged. He winced and yelled in pain as I grabbed a nipple and gave it a twist.

"Ouch, that hurt!" He smiled, "But I like you doing that to me."

I could see that he was ready to go further. I rolled over and went down on his magnificent, erect, penis. I seized his shaft and pulled down the foreskin, exposing a glistening purple tip that I flicked with my tongue before taking the full length in my mouth. He came in salty glugs that I swallowed greedily. He moaned with delight.

"I've never come in a lady's mouth before," he said. "Thank you."

"It's your turn to pleasure me now," I invited.

I started masturbating, but with the pre-come dribbling out of me, I struggled for purchase. I rubbed my hands on the bedsheet and tried again before John gently moved my hands away and took me in his mouth. My God, he was so soft. It felt almost like he had no teeth, so good was he at hiding them away as he moved up and down, up and down. It felt incredible and was possibly the best blow job I had ever had. But hard as I was, I couldn't come. I withdrew from his mouth and touched myself again. He watched me with a happy look of expectation.

I started to feel my climax mounting. "Suck me again," I gasped. "Oh God, oh God!" I shouted as pleasure pulsed through me.

I lay on the bed, panting, spent, happy. John knelt over me, a slightly gormless grin on his face, come dribbling down his chin.

"John," I paused as I registered what I was about to ask, "I want you to take me up the bum."

He groaned with desire. "Oh, I want to," he said, "but I'm not as young as I was. I don't think I can get hard again. Next time. I promise."

He lay down beside me. We cuddled. He squeezed me.

"You're all woman for me, Emma. You know that."

I kissed him again, pushing my tongue in deep. Now

I knew there was no going back. God, I loved this man!

Kevin

I was surprised when Kevin said he wanted to go for a drink with Emma. And, to be honest, I felt a bit conflicted about it. I thought long and hard about what to wear before settling on a motorsport T-shirt, denim skirt, and low-heeled boots. No full make-up either, just a powder foundation and a quick allocation of blusher. I looked at myself in the mirror. I looked good. I felt good.

We met in our usual real ale pub. Kevin stood up as I walked in, made as if to give me a hug, but then changed his mind at the last minute. I expected it would take time for him to get used to Emma.

We didn't say much to begin with. It felt so awkward that I thought about making my excuses and going home. But I decided to stay when Kevin belatedly realised that it was his round and asked what I wanted.

"I'll have a pint of Landlord, please," I said.

"A pint? I thought you were drinking halves because it was more feminine?"

"Well, I thought that too. Then I went for a drink with my friend Michelle, and I thought, if she can, so can I. There's no good reason why women can't drink pints, is there?"

"I suppose not," Kevin agreed as he headed for the bar.

I took a sip of the pint, enjoying the feel of the foamy head on my upper lip, thinking with a smile about my new adventures with my mouth.

"I guess I was wrong about people like you," Kevin said. "You're just people like any of us. And you, Emma, you're okay. I'm glad that we can still be friends." After another moment of silence, he continued, "I don't know if you're still interested in football now that you're a girl, but I've got a spare ticket for a week on Saturday."

"Of course I'm still interested in football. Why wouldn't I be?"

"Dunno. Just wondered. So, you're coming then?"

I smiled. "Is this a date?"

"No, it bloody well isn't. Drink your beer and behave!"

We both laughed.

Horny Old Woman

BY JOY MOATES

Content: ageing and sexuality, ageism, body confidence, sexual empowerment, self-celebration

Here I am… lying on my bed, my naked body feels so sweet with soft sheets barely covering her. Propped up on pillows with a glass of blood-red wine in my hand. I take a sip, feeling its delicious wetness touch my lips and then slide into my mouth. My body feels just as wet and lush as the wine. Here I am… my body languidly relaxing. She feels soft and oh-so satisfied, blissful, radiating a contented energy that she adores. Another sip of wine as I stretch my body, feeling sweetness all over. My body remembers his touch, his desire matching my own, the intensity of our fucking and, as she remembers, I sigh deeply. Ahhhh, yes. He, my young lover, was just what I needed.

I want to tell you my truth. I am woman. I am filled with wild, intuitive feminine energy. I am a highly sexual woman and I love it. You might call me a sexual/sensual junkie… a touch junkie. My sexual energy is my lifeblood. A river of eroticism flows deep in my bones.

What some might consider strange about my truth is this: I am 71 years old. I am a lustful, sexy 71-year-old woman who adores sex and who has lovers, most of them much younger than me. That is my truth. There, I said it. Sometimes the truth is difficult to say out loud. But you know what? It feels fucking good when I do.

I didn't know it would be so hard to just be me... to just be this horny woman as I aged. I didn't realise that I would face criticism and even ostracism. Perhaps even more frightening, I have to face my own fears of ageing.

This truth wasn't hard to say when I was younger. In fact, I loved saying it. It seems that all of a sudden, when I turned 70, I found myself in a box. An old-age prison and I wasn't quite sure how I got there. Where is my free-spirited wild woman? She is right under my skin... still sensuous, sexy, feeling pleasure, trusting magic and desire... yet she feels as if she's been silenced. She's scared to come out of the box. Scared that maybe it's not safe to say out loud who she is, what she wants, and how she is living. To be authentic. To be truthful.

But now, this wild woman has decided it is time to rebel. Once more, time to own her sexuality. My sexuality. My desire to have wild abandoned sex, and a wild abandoned life, for as long as I want. My decision. My life. So, I have said it out loud to all of you.

How to age with wild woman abandon? This is a question I have been asking myself a lot lately. It seems to grow more difficult with every passing year to give myself permission to be wild, sexy and sensual... as an old woman of 71. Society says it is just not happening. We hear voices around us all the time that say old women aren't sexy. Old women don't even want sex, much less enjoy it. It's gross to see an old woman acting sexy. You're too old to do pole dancing... to lust for passionate sex... to wear that clingy, short, red dress... to flirt outrageously... to say exactly what you want. The critical voices just go on and on... Do you also hear all those shrieking voices in your head? Seems the tamed ones are always telling us how to live.

Why do many think there are rules we should ALL follow as soon as we are considered old? Why would we listen to rules now if we have never listened to rules in the past? Why would we begin to walk the tamed path if we have never walked it before? There seem to be so many rules as we age, that we could spend our entire days/lives just trying to keep up with them. No pleasure in that!

They're not only unsettling and irritating; if we let them, they can stop us from living a rich, luscious, sensual life for all our years... prevent us from claiming our pleasures until we take our last breath. Sensuality and sexuality do not have an "expired by" date, I promise you. Yet it takes some work to believe that, considering all the stories we have been told. But I know it can be done. (Though I'm still working on those voices in my own head.) I know that, no matter our age, we can be juicy, sexy and sensual until the day we die. And yes, it may not look or feel like it did when we were 30, 40 or even 50, yet it is still true in all its deliciously sexy glory. Just because we have aged doesn't mean we don't still get to own our sexuality. We get to choose how we use it, how we show up with it, who we share it with. It is our life, our choice, our sexuality... just as it was when we were younger. And it takes rebelling against society's norms. In our culture, living a sexual, sensual life filled with pleasure, at any age but especially at old age, is an act of rebellion.

I've always been a highly sexual woman (beginning in my teens). Even at a young age, I found my body to be my friend... I loved her and she allowed me to feel so many pleasures. And I seldom felt guilty about any of those pleasures. In fact, not only did my sex and sexual pleasures bring me (and my partners) immense joy, but I also learned many life lessons through my intimate sexual relationships. They were powerful and often healing.

I was an embodied woman long before I knew the term "embodied". I felt my way through life, through my world. I was in touch with all of my senses and used them to not only bring me pleasure, but to help me navigate through my world... and to help me navigate through myself... learning who I was... am. The erotic in all its forms has always called to me, enticed me. My erotic language is lust, sensual, and kink. I have had an adventurous, passionate sex life filled with two husbands and many lovers. At different times in my life, I have been polyamorous, and monogamous; I've practised serial monogamy and enjoyed rendezvous with strangers. My desire for wild, passionate fucking has never left me. It is one of my core values and something I need. A delicious sexy life is vital to my physical, mental and emotional health. At least for now. I sometimes wonder if my desire will last into my 80s. I certainly hope so and will do my best to ensure that I stay turned on to sex and to life itself. I do not want to deny my sexual hunger.

Maybe you can understand how odd I felt when things in my mind started to shift when I turned 70. For the first time, I began to hear the voices of a culture that said, "You can't desire sex any more, you can't be sexy and alluring, you can't dress like that, you can't even SAY that you want sex." I began to question myself for the first time ever. I have always sashayed down my own path... not worried about what others thought about it. I wasn't loud or boisterous in advertising my lifestyle, yet I didn't try to hide it. I just went about living my life, especially my sexual life, as I desired. So why then, out of the blue, did I find myself questioning why I desired the things I still desired? Society was telling me something was wrong with me, yet I didn't feel that way. Those other voices in my head were loud enough to give me pause; I had to learn to push back. And push back I have. And I invite you and all women to push back on these antiquated rules that are meant to keep us docile.

A large part of my truth and journey is embracing my ageing body, seeing all of her beauty and knowing deep in my bones that she is worthy and deserving of erotic touch. The kind of erotic touch that I desire… that turns me on.

Lately, my wild feminine has been screaming at me. She is no longer willing to be silent. She is the one who has led me for most of my life. She is the true essence of who I am. And when I listen to her, I am never led astray. But sometimes, during the past year, I have been quieting her down. Asking her if maybe we shouldn't be quite so "us"… maybe we should "act our age". And she doesn't like this at all. And I am so fucking thankful that she doesn't. Because as she always has, she is reminding me just who I really am and how I should always be authentic. Being authentic, just like being sexy, does not have an expiration date. Sometimes she screams this to me so that her voice is louder than all the crazy ones in my head. I wonder, do you have a wild woman inside you begging you to come home to your true self? To be YOU, no matter your age?

By embracing my "ageing" wild woman – or maybe my "wild old woman" – I am rebelling. I do not want to listen to how I should age gracefully. How I should drop into the background of life. I will continue to create my life in vivid colours. I desire to age with fierce abandon and that is exactly what I am going to do. I want to age as a liberated sexual woman. It's time that those of us who still have a strong libido and who desire sexual partners stand up and say it with pride. We need to talk about our lustful desires. We need to claim our right to our sexuality. At every fucking age. We are the ones who must change societal views and rigid rules. We must speak up... tell our personal truth. Yell it at the top of our lungs if necessary. Would you like to shout it with me? Let's hear it: I love sex; I desire and enjoy my lovers; I can and will find sexual pleasure my way and at any age. It is time we began a revolution of old women!

I desire to have yearnings. I desire to have passion. Those feelings of my breath catching in anticipation, feeling his hands all over me, deep yearning sighs that escape from my body, that yearning deep in my pussy, deep in my bones. Why would I want to give up all that pleasure? That pleasure, that passion, is life to me. And I feel it most with a lover. His roughness mixed with tenderness, his words of want and need as they wash over me. I choose desire and passion. I don't need companionship. I love living alone and I love being by myself. I am not lonely. I want eroticism, desire, touch, fucking with passion, with wildness. I want that connectedness with another human that is the deepest connection I can have... bodies, soul and energy. My sexual desire fuels my life, with or without lovers. It is a force that fuels my creativity. I cannot write or paint without that passion, that yearning. I don't need a hero; I don't need a partner. I do want a passionate lover or lovers. For one night or for many.

My lovers have always been younger than me. My current lover is 25. I have shared that with very few friends because many would find it disgusting, I imagine. And why is that? Why is it widely accepted that old men have young lovers but it is sick when that is reversed? When will society just let us women be? Quit telling us how we should act… and then ignore us as if we weren't even there.

I wish to normalise old women adoring sex with one or many lovers. I want to normalise older women having much younger lovers. I want to do more than just normalise. I want to make it seem magical. Have the entire world excited about it.

I have honoured my juicy sexuality all these years. And it has felt so delicious and still feels delicious. So, if this eroticism is still burning inside me, why am I made to feel that I should give it up? How absurd. I don't really need to examine the why's of my desire. I just love that it is there. That I still yearn and want. And I know that there are other women out there just like me. So, maybe if I admit it, others will join me. I hope to open discussions about old women desiring sex… and not just for companionship or intimacy. Desiring sex for the pure pleasure of having sex whenever we want and with whomever we want. Sex for the pure pleasure of having sex. I crave that intimate connection and that orgasmic bliss that I only find in sexual contact. I still love exploring and being curious about what turns me on and what turns my lover on. I never think of my age when I am with a lover. And I never think of my age when I am self-pleasuring and bringing myself to orgasm.

Because the real truth is that, for some of us, sex just keeps getting better. Even us elders enjoy wild eroticism. My body knows the truth of passion and lust and eroticism and her responsiveness is powerful. She just throws herself fully into the moment, embracing every touch, every wetness, every seduction. Free to be her sexually liberated self and enjoy her lover. Truly lost in the moment. I still find no better way to be fully embodied than through intimately and nakedly connecting with another person through sex.

And here's another truth. Desiring lovers in older age requires vulnerability and being gentle with ourselves. It's not all just passion and lust. Sometimes it is lonely. Being an introvert and not one to go out often, I have found it sometimes a challenge to find sexual partners. Dating apps and online dating services are a strange landscape to me. Maybe you feel this way also. I laughingly say that I just keep waiting for lovers to mysteriously show up at my front door. Which does happen sometimes, yet I've found you can't count on it. I found this hard to accept at first because finding lovers had never been an issue for me. But there are fewer options as we grow older. And it's not just about the times when lovers are difficult to find or even non-existent. I often feel alone in the sea of older women. Does anyone else have intense feelings of desire like I do? Crave sexual touch like I do? By sharing these feelings, we will all feel less alone.

In those times when I have no lovers, I am my own best lover. I have had to face the sad reality that I may not always have the lovers I desire. So, although I want a vibrant sex life, sometimes it's more lacklustre than vibrant. But I am always hopeful. I know that by being my own lover and satisfying my body in ways she loves, I am keeping the fires of my sexual energy alive. And that gives me a passion for life itself.

So, here I am... wondering why this deliciously decadent feeling of bliss should be wrong. Especially since we know the healing powers of intimacy and touch for all humans. Wondering why it isn't considered normal for old women to feel so luscious, so sexy, so juicy. Hell, why isn't it considered a priority? Why should it be wrong to crave this much pleasure?

I want to live in a world where women are finally liberated sexually. A world of luscious, sexy, juicy old women. A world where women, no matter how old, are free to crave, desire and enjoy the sweet pleasures of sex with their lovers or themselves – and talk about it – without being ostracised. And I will do my part to create that world. I will not deny my sexual hunger. I invite you to join me in this revolution. Young and old. We are all on our very own unique erotic journey. Let's celebrate that and say "fuck you" to a society that tells us we are no longer sexual beings. Are you with me?

As I step into this journey of ageing with wild abandon, I know that my journey will grow and evolve as I do. I have taken enough journeys through writing, painting and life to understand that we never fully know how our path will wander. Yet, I do know this path will be filled with sensuality and eroticism. Will you walk this path, your path, with me?

You Say I'm Too Old

You say that I'm too old to feel eroticism
To feel sexual
But what of this heat I feel between my legs
This wetness dripping down my thighs
These breasts that are swelling
Nipples aching to be touched
What of that?
How can I be too old if my body
desires so much?

What are you afraid of?
Are you scared to look at a body
that holds the scars of a life well lived?
A body that has seen more passion
than you can even imagine?
A body that may not look like your version of sexy
And just what is YOUR version of sexy?
And why the fuck should that be
everyone's version of sexy?

Or maybe, you are afraid of the force of my erotic fire
The power that I wield with this arousing energy
This compelling sexual energy that all women have,
no matter their age
Are you frightened
Is that it?

Or maybe you're just afraid that you will yield
to the seduction of my eroticism
Or that you'll give in to the temptation
of becoming amorous yourself
When everyone else is saying, oh,
you're much too old for that!

This, too, is Intimacy

BY ESTHER WILD

Content: caregiving (children and ageing parents), perimenopause, endometriosis

Shivering, damp and clammy, I gather the covers closely around my shoulders. My body has begun to generate a heat I don't recognise. This nightly dance of sweaty wakefulness and constant movement has become an unwelcome routine as I search for a dry, clean, comfortable spot in the bed, my hair drenched, cold, and sticky, my skin coated in a salty sheen.

I recall a different kind of midnight heat, a ravenous wakefulness that was always worth the payback of daytime fatigue.

Now I ache to rest, restore, and find some reserves to carry on another day.

I fall back into a shallow, snoring slumber, woken at 5 a.m. with a phone call as my mum's dementia casts a veil over linear time.

The all too familiar tension is already occupying space in our bed, a space in which a playful closeness used to have room to spark and flourish.

My tired body is set rigidly in a functional freeze, locking out the fire of eroticism.

My mind, full of imminent tasks and challenges of the hours ahead, somehow can't map out a clear path amongst the dense, swirling fog that lurks where my smart, sharp brain used to be.

Sensuality is forgotten, just another task on the to-do list, and one that got left far, far behind in priorities.

There is already a mountain of things to do.

I stumble between trying to look after my mum, our teenage daughters, a household and working life, while at every moment the hormones that used to keep my skin plump, my belly flatter, and my libido high are rushing to leave, not even a backwards glance on the way out.

My body and soul long for downtime, for deep rest, space and self-connection – all of which feels like an entire dimension away from the one in which I fucked.

I ask the younger me how I did it.

How did I find that drive, that primal need, a gloriously wild, insatiable inner fire?

I don't hear her answer.

I can't imagine how she would view this bloated, exhausted future self, whose daily ambition is to get as much rest as possible and maybe some alone time.

I just long for my bed, alone, with every sinew and cell of my being.

Scrolling through my phone to find mindless relief, social media boasts to me of women my age who are in their "siren era", owning their Queenage power, showing us all how their sexuality is front and centre, proudly baring breast and pussy power slogans on their grids.

I bet they don't have to call the hospital and wait on hold, or do the shopping for two households today, I think.

Fucking feels like a lifetime ago.

The moments of flirting, anticipation, touch, and prolonged closeness don't even enter my awareness as the day flies from to-do lists to tiredness in one long yawn.

As one extra task turns into another day spent chasing down medication, connecting departments, and trying to keep up with laundry loads amongst snatched periods of work, I begin to sob.

Society doesn't make space for the women who were told in the '90s that we could have it all.

The ladettes are exhausted, bleeding oestrogen into the ether of emotional load, and collapsing under the weight of being sandwiched between generations.

I make my way back to bed, searching for the comfort of covers and the mirage of sleep.

In my late teens and twenties, I ran from intimacy, seeking love, approval and connection by role-playing pleasure and abandon for radically undeserving men.

My womb responded to the self-sabotage and soul violations with endometriosis, a barbed wire chastity belt overridden with alcohol, puncturing my divine feminine sacral source with piercing pain, an alarm system that took me years to finally hear.

Ah. That's how I did it. Desire was manufactured, performative, soulless. Erotica ruled but without connection.

I was following the tacit guidebook of faux feminine empowerment, where claiming our seat at the table meant becoming all things to men whilst denying and decrying our own power.

Decades after I traded empty sex and wounded relationships for the deep love of a soul mate, I lie beside him in my shattered, vulnerable state and feel the warmth of his hand in mine.

This, too, is intimacy.

The man who has been by my side through the births of our children, the death of one parent and the dementia demise of another. A lover who is consistent, present and real, no matter which season of life we are in.

This is an intimacy that lives in our daily affection, the trust, friendship and respect that grows and thrives while we white knuckle the twists and turns of humanity together.

When sex joins us, it's a gift, a connection that's always accompanied by wondering why we don't do this more.

And then the need for rest and renewal returns.

Erotica lives quietly in the midlife, middle-eight of this season, for me.

Intimacy takes on a deeper form.

Both, I know, await a new chapter that I long to write, as I take a glance towards my third act.

Talk About the Passion: Confessions of an Insatiable, Demisexual Slut

BY JULES PURNELL

Content: COVID-19, kink, pleasure activism

I've always been a passion-driven animal. I don't just need to fuck; I need to eat, to taste the blood, to feel bone with my teeth, tongue the marrow, grip the flesh with my claws, and swallow with my whole heart. My erotic imagination and appetite have always been vast, back into the memories of my early childhood. I'm not a casual consumer, nor am I usually content with small samples. I love the feeling of being consumed, and I appreciate lovers who can meet me there. The initial surge of my relationships tends to be full of creativity, exploration, a sparkling vitality of desire, devotion, and mutual sense of adventure. Sex feels like play, cavorting in the unabashed nakedness of the Garden of Eden. What Rimbaud meant when he spoke of, "those woods where sex was once a children's game."[1]

Oftentimes, the sheer volume of my eroticism (and accompanying invitation into the erotic) can help inspire it in my partners. I make living into desire look so tantalisingly good that it becomes its own seduction. Sex is also my profession, a considerable portion of that being a professional slut, a beacon of sexuality. No matter the medium, the invitation remains the same: "Want me, see me, touch me..." I've curated this kind of persona for a purpose. I wear it as a badge of honour as much as a warning. I want my would-be suitors to know what they're getting themselves into.

This persona is not a put-on; it's a key part of who I am. My sexuality is close to my holiness, is close to my carnality, is close to my power. To touch it, to be in conversation with it is to be in what feels like the truest forms of myself. When others misunderstand it, cheapening it into something shameful or frivolous, they miss the point altogether. Not only can it not be diminished, to attempt to smother it with shame or accusations of "too much"-ness is like attempting to break the spirit of a wild animal. The coloniser's fear of the untamed is just that; a fear misplaced because he cannot comprehend what it means to truly be free himself. He can't imagine a world without captivity.

Part of my way of being in the world is a kind of pleasure activism[2]; I firmly believe the machinations of capitalism want us to be disconnected from our bodies and disconnected from one another, because in that state we doubt our power and deny our own humanity. Our bodies and the collective wisdom they hold when they connect with the bodies of others is the source of our liberation. It fits into my politics to seek sexual pleasure (as well as other forms of leisure and enjoyment) for its own sake, to undo the religious exhortations that we feel ashamed of our joy, that we're only holy when we suffer. Some people aren't along for this ride quite yet. And so, those who have felt inadequate because they can't keep up with me (or have been punished into distrusting their own sexuality, deprioritising their own pleasure) have tried in vain to project their fear and shame onto me. But the sheer force of my sacred sexuality can't be squelched; it has a mind and a soul and a life of its own.

Alongside the libidinal excitement I draw out of others, there is still more to me, and some have gotten confused here too. I am more than just fantasy. I am fantasy; make no mistake. I try to live as close to fantasy embodied as I am able. It is true that I am perhaps the best sex and the most affirming, accepting, and satisfying experience in the sexual realm many have known. I have considerable skills and talents, (thank god for sex work, no?) as well as a heart that craves to know the desires of your heart as well. What I offer is not just a mutual generosity beyond GGG (good, giving, and game), but an emotionally enveloping soft space to land. You will inadvertently admit things to me you haven't admitted to anyone else, perhaps not even yourself. I will unlock things you didn't know lay dormant. You will feel held and nourished when you do so and I, in turn, vow to never abuse this power. (Unless that's part of the game.) It is a power; I wield it with great care, and with the recognition of the solemnity my role in this dance demands. I am an entrusted custodian of this desire, and I tend this holy temple like any other devoted observant.

But I am also whole... I am not a Manic Pixie Dream Slut, here to merely serve as your point of sexual self-actualisation. I am complicated, I am often moody, I am imperfect, constantly growing and learning, and I am a creature of great emotional need. I am just as romantically inclined as I am sexually inclined and my desire skews towards both. I'm a big, bold force of nature. My standards are high all the way around (I demand a lot of my lovers) and shrinking myself has never done me or any of my lovers any good.

Because the truth of who I am always becomes self-evident, always swells, grows big, bigger than the container of sheer fantasy can withstand.

When the complexity of my being and the demands of day-to-day life temper my sexual relationships, they inevitably tend to reach some kind of a cooling. This is normal. Most relationships, most people, settle into a kind of sweetness and warmth when the heat dials down in a long-term, committed relationship. However, beyond stability and comfort, familiarity can breed a kind of complacency. This was true especially when the entire world hit the pause button on itself, on so many recognisable forms of commerce, on nearly all forms of human contact during the rise of what we would all come to know as the novel Coronavirus COVID-19, now simply called COVID.

In March of 2020, I held a play party with close friends of mine, renting a cabin in the Poconos for a weekend of fun and debauchery. The following week as the news of the spreading virus broke, many of us were sent home from our jobs, unsure of how long it would be until we returned. We cocooned ourselves in with our nearest and dearest – if we had significant others or families at all. I count those of us who did as lucky; many struggled alone without even a pod of acquaintances to share refuge and company. But for me, a funny thing happened... As my beloved partner and I turned inward, with presumably more time, access, and ability to be with one another, (a potential bonus of suddenly working from home and being unable to leave our house) the heat we once knew abandoned us altogether. We used to welcome the experience of getting marooned together, of being cloistered away from the world, but suddenly that felt hard to embrace.

Our courtship started hot and heavy against the winter

chill in early December of 2017. We would intentionally get snowed in together, making dates for the night before a big storm, hoping it meant our respective jobs would be cancelled the next day. We eagerly spent those days exploring and devouring one another, in between making breakfast and lounging with their (and now my) children. For many years I had ached for a balance between the hedonistic and domestic, and in truth, I still feel incomplete when one or the other of them is missing. As wild and untamed as my libido can be, I am as much a sucker for the hearth and home. It felt like real bliss.

Fast forward to some years on, and between a global pandemic and the onslaught of a fascist presidential regime (whose spirit-crushing daily inundation cannot ever be overstated) our spark had all but died. At a time when I would have loved to turn towards each other and take comfort in each other's bodies, we quietly and abruptly turned away. We barely touched each other for months. We were working, parenting, cohabiting automatons whose sexual connection had died on the vine. We weren't even sleeping in the same bed; I took up temporary residence in our basement in-law's suite. My own connection to my sexual and kinky self slipped into a quiet coma, and I attempted (and failed) to jumpstart it by flirting with strangers online and exchanging slutty photos with friends.

Meanwhile, I wasn't sleeping. I was caught up in a wave of pandemic-flavoured, panic-addled insomnia the likes of which I've never experienced before. I've dealt with insomnia my entire adult life, but this was a whole new animal. My eyes conjured figures from the dark of my bedroom, insisting that something was waiting for me behind every door. My mind materialised an amorphous threat crouching behind every piece of furniture. Some nights, when I tried in vain to masturbate myself to sleep, I fantasised about a stranger coming into my basement bedroom to ravage me, fantasies no doubt informed by my rabid true crime consumption. I begged for even my darkest, pandemic-spun demons to be my rescuers from the dullness of my ailing libido... If the things that go bump in the night wouldn't kill me, the least they could do was fuck me when they visited. I waded through my days in a sleep-deprived fog, dreading the coming nights.

I decided I couldn't let this be my life any longer. Once COVID vaccination (and subsequent boosters) became a viable possibility and the world that had shuttered itself began to open back up, my partner and I discussed re-open-ing our relationship in turn. We had started our relation-ship as non-monogamous both in theory and in practice, but after a long reprieve, (and a libido that was aching for co-conspirators) I knew it was time to re-engage. My sex drive has always been too much to put on one person to satisfy, and after many months of complaint and fears that I was breathing down my partner's neck to meet my needs, I decided to outsource my horniness. I got back on the dating apps in earnest and began courting new dates.

However, this my partner and I could not weather – I'm sad to say, after almost two years of trying, our relationship did not survive. It was one of the darkest chapters of my life to admit at long last that this once blissful relationship had to come to an end. Blowing up my entire life, I moved out, took a new lover, courted a handful of new dates, hosted kinky play parties, invited friends and strangers to see slutty selfies on a new sex-positive Instagram account, (a creative and often losing proposition in the face of increas-ing online censorship) and did what I could to resuscitate my voracious, sexual self. I made promises that I would never go back, could never go back to being a person who ignored my needs and desires.

The year is now 2024. COVID is still with us, a lingering ghost that we may never fully shake; like HIV that came before it, still with us but less a harbinger of immediate death than it once was. Like everyone, through lockdown and in the years since, I have undergone many changes to the very concept of my own person. I came out of quarantine a stranger to myself in many ways, a whole new version of myself I'm still getting to know. At 39 years old, I find myself asking, "Who am I?" in ways that I never have. A creature of perpetual reinvention, this position is both familiar yet altogether new.

Having sated my hunger for the proverbial "more," (I've gotten my hands on plenty of new flesh on this side of the lockdown) I find myself newly navigating a sexual desire that demands emotional connection in tandem with the sexual. Always a romantic, I now find that experiences of sex that don't include deep, loving feelings leave me cold. For a while I kept trying, chasing the dragon of excitement I had once felt in casual sex, but after a handful of unsatisfying experiences, I have to simply admit that that's not who I am at this point in my life. Even with recurring, known partners (who were absolutely lovely but not loving-relationship material) I was never able to feel the itch fully scratched. I crave surrender, relinquishment, and a devotion that can only be given from a place of depth of connection.

I'm currently exploring what it might mean to be demisexual, a person who requires emotional connection prior to feeling fully present and fulfilled in a sexual experience. To complicate matters, I'm also in a stable and loving relationship with a partner who defines their sexual orientation as grey ace – a first for me, as I've never dated anyone who outwardly names themself as part of the asexual spectrum before. How do I square a burgeoning demi identity with the insatiable, libidinal impulse that lives so loud in me? Like, yes, I want to be a slut, but only with people who can meet me in spiritual, kinky, loving communion as well.

Some months ago, my grey ace partner and I started out hot and heavy, as my relationships almost always do, but have since settled into a softer, gentler union. They admitted to me that they weren't sure what existed of their ace-ness, having not had the chance to beta test it in quite a while. Upon our first meeting, (coinciding with the first time we fucked) that question seemed to be put to rest for us both. At first long distance and electric, (literally and figuratively; most of our interactions were facilitated by smartphone, laptop, and Bluetooth-capable vibrators) we are currently navigating what it means to occasion the spark we once had, now that we spend considerably more time together and have less ability to cultivate strangeness with one another. Esther Perel teaches us that distance is what creates intrigue, which in turn invites eroticism.[3] Yet I found long-distance dating intolerable on an attachment-style-demoralising, nervous-system-dysregulating level. I yearned for the days when we could be together to act out our fantasies in the flesh, but somehow, it has felt remote and hard to access in the here and now.

Don't get me wrong; we have great sex. I climax more consistently than I maybe ever have. The frequency isn't lacking. The sex is not the problem, per se. As the text by surrogate partner Dr. Tova Feder advises, "Sex is the least of it."[4] I want the exploration, the boldness, the admission of "I've always wanted to try..." I want the coy invitation, coming home to a nude body on the bed waiting to be devoured, the bared neck begging for teeth, the pursuit, the fulfilment, the rapture, the un-doneness that passionate, exploratory sex brings. I want to be in partnership in ways that co-create a sexual script using a shared language that perhaps is yet undiscovered. I want to worship at one another's temples, acolytes in a religion of two.[5]

And so, I wind up here again, asking myself the questions I have been asking for my entire adult life: How do I balance the desire for the kind of kinetic, frenetic sexuality my libido craves with the thirst for pastoral domesticity our current modern era of romance and post-agrarian capitalism encourages?[6] How do I live into my slutitude while respecting the boundaries of my partners (having zero interest in half-hearted, acquiescent sex)? Why is it that almost everyone I've dated experiences a dip in libido as the relationship progresses, but mine never quite seems to do so? Moving forward, do I prioritise sexual connection over all other aspects of a relationship, knowing what a central cause of friction it has been? And how do I make sense of a sexual appetite that now requires a depth of loving feeling like it never has before?

I wish I had the answer. I wish I knew what came next. Trying to get this ending tidy feels like a losing proposition. I commit to remaining curious, and to keeping the promises I made to myself to never, ever go back to ignoring what and who I need to be in this world. I am, after all, my most consistent sex partner and my longest relationship. The key tattooed on my left ring finger reminds me every day of the commitment I made to myself as my own primary partner. Everyone else is welcome to leave an offering at the altar.

1   Arthur Rimbaud, Animals Once Spewed Semen (Paul Schmidt transla-
     tion, 1975)

2   adrienne maree brown, Pleasure Activism: The Politics of Feeling Good,
     2019

3   Esther Perel, Mating In Captivity: Unlocking Erotic Intelligence, 2017

4   Tova Feder, Sex Is the Least of It: Surrogate Partners Discuss Love Life
     and Intimacy, 2014

5   Being non-monogamous by orientation, I still honor that each dyad
     creates its own unique world, and sometimes its own religion within it.

6   Don't get me started on the connection between agriculture, domestic-
     ity, the Nuclear family, and patriarchy.

Don't You Want Me?

BY LILY JENKINS

Content: *libido, perimenopause, penetration, reconnecting with an old flame*

At forty-seven years of age, Louise had never expected to be celibate. Especially not within a marriage. Twenty years ago, she and her husband had talked about still making love in their eighties, and joked about how they would need to be careful so as not to break a hip! It would appear that this was not to be the case, however.

She was trying to figure out when it had all changed: when had their sex life gone from healthy, regular and playful to now non-existent? Their last act of sexual intimacy was pre-pandemic. Louise tried to recall whether things were dwindling before then, and maybe they were – parenting teenagers and both working full-time didn't leave a great amount of space to be together, but they managed it and enjoyed it when it happened. They had been creative in the bedroom (and other rooms, she remembered with a smile...), they had played together, experimented and brought each other pleasure. He had been open to trying bondage, allowing her to bind his wrists to the bedstead and blindfold him, giving her free rein in taking the lead. She had given him permission to dominate too, waiting for him on the bed, kneeling, wrists cuffed behind her back. They had trusted each other. And outside of that, there was physical intimacy, sharing a close space. Touching and holding each other, flirtatious glances and comments, even public kissing.

When had all that stopped?

To rub salt into the wound, perimenopause had brought with it not only the joys of hot flushes, brain fog, anxiety, occasional bouts of inexplicable rage, and the belief she was losing her mind, but also an increase in her libido. Not just a little bit: Louise's libido was on steroids. There were days when she felt so horny, she thought she might cry. She could be at work, in the supermarket, driving, there was no clear trigger or warning, but the feelings of desire and sexual need were, on some days, overwhelming. The knot of desire in her abdomen grew tighter and tighter, heat rose through her core demanding her attention, it was an itch that she couldn't scratch.

Where were the warnings about this? When women or experts talked about menopause, they always talked about a lack of libido, of sex drives switching off, women no longer wanting an intimate relationship with their partners. Certainly, all the friends she had discussed it with fell on that side of the fence. If she did too, that would have been a gift! It would no longer matter that her marriage was now a sex-free zone. As it was, Louise's libido felt like it had downed a hefty dose of amphetamine and was determined to take centre stage. It felt like a flamboyant performer wearing a sequined cloak, stepping out of the dry ice smoke, and demanding to be acknowledged and sated. But – Louise thought sadly – she was a performer without an audience.

So, here she was, negotiating a new phase in her life, trying to embrace stepping into midlife with all its accompanying changes: the wisdom and experience she had gained over the years, feeling slightly less pressure to conform, and finding more time for herself. She was also grieving – mourning the loss of marital intimacy – and longing to be desired.

It is a cruel twist of fate, Louise thought, that so many losses come at the same time of life. On reaching nearly fifty, women often have to manage their children flying the nest – she was certainly struggling with this. A new phase of motherhood, letting go of her once small children into the big wide world, no longer needed or relied upon so heavily. No longer the centre of their world, the love of their life, their provider and nurturer. She was also having to face the fact that her parents were older. They were not going to be around forever, and that thought was too much for her to face. Her career was going well, she had climbed the ladder as much as she had wanted to, but the thought of another twenty years working in this job was exhausting. Financially, she was in a stronger position than her husband, and the weight of this responsibility was tiring.

And then there was the loss of her younger self. Not loss, perhaps, maybe the evolution of her. The not knowing who she was without the label of 'mum'. This seemed to Louise to be the perfect time for her relationship to move into a new phase, a time for reconnection. More time for them as a couple, more space, more freedom. Instead of quickies in the kitchen, they could be taking time to explore each other without the fear of interruption. She had imagined lazy weekend mornings in bed, lying together, playing together, being close and renewing their physical bond. But, so far, that wasn't to be.

For months now, the answer was always 'no'. Verbally or physically, her husband made it clear that he wasn't interested in physical intimacy. Hugs became... just less. He no longer wrapped his arms around her to draw her to him, rather, he stood stiffly as she tried to get closer to him. The loss of communication between them was like an abyss. She had tried subtlety. She had tried being playful, attempting in a light-hearted way to dance seductively with him, moving her hips against him and being overtly flirtatious. She had tried bluntly asking, "Do you miss sex?" "No," had been the reply. At one point, she had almost begged: kneeling on the floor next to the sofa, on the verge of tears, after he had pushed her away from him. She rested her forehead on his thigh and asked, "Why don't you want me any more? Please, tell me what's going on. I need you. I miss you." All she got in return was a raised barrier. He focused on the television and said he had "some stuff to work through." It felt as though he didn't trust her with his private thoughts any more.

At a time when she was losing so much of who she felt she was, losing the role of lover was painful. She felt desperate for affection, attention, and acknowledgement. She felt starved of touch and tenderness. She needed connection.

Perimenopause had taken Louise by surprise and the past six months had been a rollercoaster of emotions that had started like the flick of a switch. At one point, she really did think she was going mad. She became highly anxious, paranoid, easily tearful. She felt completely disconnected from her loved ones at times, as if she was walking through their worlds like an unseen entity, an outside observer. She had felt like a failure at work, an imposter attempting to play the highly skilled role she was in. Her brain felt like it was walking through treacle. She couldn't sleep at night but took naps that lasted hours because she was exhausted. And the rage! Not often, but Louise struggled with this the most. Untriggered, unbidden, it would overtake her and she could find no outlet except to walk it off. She couldn't be around people for fear of what she might say or do.

On one particular morning, she had woken wearing this veil of rage. She had stomped around the house, not daring to speak to anyone. It stayed with her throughout the morning, causing her to walk out of a meeting at work as her agitation and irritability threatened to overspill. She needed reassurance, she needed to be understood. Louise was struggling.

Amid the chaos, she needed to come back to herself. Louise had spent many years working on knowing she was enough, just as she was, away from the male gaze and without the pressure of external expectations. She had unlearned so much body image bullshit and had come to a place where she accepted her body for what it allowed her to do rather than what it looked like. She had learned to appreciate her curves; the first step had been to buy a full-length mirror. She no longer quickly applied moisturiser to her body after a shower, Louise now made a point of standing in front of the mirror while she gently and lovingly smoothed the skin of her limbs and torso with a luxurious body butter. She would consciously watch herself give her body some much-needed love and gratitude. She would smile at her reflection instead of hiding from it, ignoring it, or criticising it.

She had learned to be thankful for her now softer, rounder belly. Her body had grown and fed healthy children, and Louise had punished it by restricting food, purging, and undertaking gruelling exercise. It had taken a long time to learn how to nourish and take care of herself again in that respect. She had started to learn how to exist for her own happiness and comfort rather than for the pleasure and approval of others. But now, the feeling of rejection from a man whom she had shared so much of her life with, who she loved, had shaken that new-found confidence.

She had gained a little weight when she stopped restricting herself – he assured her that wasn't the reason for his detachment. He said he still found her attractive. So why didn't he want her? With no answer forthcoming, Louise's doubts crept in, and she started craving attention from other sources to boost her sense of self-worth. Her thoughts began to revert to the time when male approval was essential to her, despite her knowing deep down that she was enough.

And then there was Max. Louise had known Max for... could it really be nearly thirty years? They had met through a mutual friend whilst Louise was at university. Max was a few years older than her, but they had hit it off immediately, and although no long-term relationship ever developed, they were fuck buddies for many years. Their rendezvous had not been regular – two or three times a year maybe – but the physical connection they had was explosive. Louise had had sexual partners before Max, but he was the first to bring her to orgasm. He knew how to fuck. He taught her more about her body, about where and how she liked to be touched, than she had ever known before she met him. Just the thought of him aroused her. Even now, she could bring to mind the touch of his fingertips running along her spine. She could feel his breath against her neck as he gently kissed her, his lips softly skimming the skin of her collarbones. She could imagine his hands tracing her waist, moving downward toward her eager centre.

Max.

The last time she had seen him was not long after she had met her husband. A chance meeting in a shopping mall. Max had looked as he always did: tall and lean, unshaven, and casually dressed in jeans and a T-shirt. She had introduced him to her not-yet-husband as an old friend from university. As the two men made small talk, Louise watched Max, remembering their most recent meeting six months before. His place, his couch. The untouched coffee he had made her that was cold by the time they stopped for breath. Their well-practised dance of undressing whilst consuming each other with their lips, their tongues hungrily searching for each other. Their hands exploring familiar territory; the rhythm of their desires matching perfectly. She had sat astride him on the couch, her hands on his knees behind her to retain some balance. Max's mouth on her breast, one hand at the small of her back, the other deliciously teasing her clit as her spine snaked to move her back and forth, his cock deep inside her. As her body shuddered to its climax, she could feel her flesh pulsating around him, and as she fell forward with her arms around his shoulders, his release quickly followed.

The brief meeting in the shopping mall had ended with a handshake for her not-yet-husband and an embrace for her, maybe a few seconds too long. He had whispered in her ear, "Don't forget me."

Max.

* * *

They had last made contact via text about eighteen months ago. They had kept in touch in a platonic way – an occasional holiday snap, a "Happy Christmas" message, a "Hello, how are you doing?" But their exchanges had been nothing more than just friendly for many years. She had no idea where he was living now, or whether he was single or not.

Would he want to see her? Would he still want her?

Contacting him now would be madness. Her rational brain knew that but her hormone-addled, desire-filled mind was not being rational. It was desperate. Desperate for her desire to be reciprocated, to feel the touch and raw sexual want of another person. She wanted to lose herself in a moment of hedonism, for her senses to take over and to experience the release she longed for.

But at what cost?

Her marriage, for all its faults, was not awful. Was it worth risking twenty years of a relationship, of all their shared history, for sex? They had a good life, a good home, they could afford to be reasonably comfortable. She and her husband, on the whole, had a happy marriage. They got on together. They were settled.

Was it worth risking her children's stability? Yes, they were grown up now, living their own lives and spreading their wings, but home was still their home, their roots. To tear that from under them would be cruel. She couldn't bear the thought of them hating her.

Or her husband hating her.

Selfish.

Who was she to even consider breaking what they had?

She was the woman who had given all of herself to her family and her career for two decades. Who had put herself second, third, and last on the list, to make sure everyone else was happy. Who had sacrificed any free time she may have had to the children's sports clubs and art clubs; making sure lunches were ready and uniforms were clean. Making sure they all had what they needed. She had been a full-time employee, a full-time mother, a full-time home-maker. Surely now was her time? Now that Louise only had herself to be responsible for, couldn't she focus on her own happiness? Why should it be so wrong?

For four years, she had been patient and tried to be understanding. She was tired of always trying. She was tired of being rejected over and over again. She was tired of feeling invisible. Louise wanted someone to see her, to bear witness to her existence.

* * *

One morning, it happened.

It was a normal day, nothing out of the ordinary, but something in her snapped and her mind said, "Fuck it." She pulled her phone from her pocket as she walked from the car park to the office and scrolled through to Max's number.

Hey x

She sent their usual greeting.

A few minutes passed before her phone pinged a response:

Well, hey! How's you, stranger? x x

She smiled to herself as she sat down at her desk. How should she play this?

Oh, you know, living the dream! How are you? x

Moments felt like hours waiting for a reply. She walked to the coffee machine to occupy herself. By the time she sat back down with her latte, he had responded.

Am OK. Better for hearing from you… When are you free? It's been far too long x x

Her pulse began to race, her palms felt clammy.

Let me check my diary and get back to you. Evening drink? x

Sounds good. Speak soon x x
Fuck.

The rest of the work day went by in a daze. There were meetings and emails but Louise's focus was elsewhere.
"It's been far too long."
When she got back to her car at 5:30, Louise looked at her phone again. An evening drink. They could never do just an evening drink. They had never managed the social, friend-zone relationship. Theirs had always been an intense, passionate one. Not much talking about mundane day-to-day activities, always straight to the part where they were removing each other's clothing. Early in their time together, when they thought they could date, they had tried to have a meal out. Nice restaurant, nice food, too much nice wine. They had planned to go their separate ways after the meal, a goodnight kiss on the pavement before hailing a taxi for her. Instead, they found themselves in the hotel next door to the restaurant, the goodnight kiss morphing into so much more. The door to the hotel room had barely closed before Max had her up against the wall, her arse pressing against his straining crotch. With his lips on her neck, he slid his hand between her thighs. His fingers easily slipped inside her, and he rhythmically worked his thumb against her engorged clit while her hips moved against him. With his other hand, Max unbuckled his belt and released his cock from his jeans. He was fully aroused. He tugged her underwear aside and was inside her cunt with a single thrust. Louise gasped as he filled her and allowed him to move deeper and deeper inside her, groaning as the coiled spring in her abdomen wound tighter and tighter. Her body collapsed between the wall and Max as she came, crying out with pleasure and release. Max came too, with

one final thrust inside her and a moan in her ear. Then he carried her to the bed, where they lay still fully clothed, as their breathing slowed to a normal rate. Louise rested her head on his chest as Max stroked her hair, feeling his heart still pounding.

She was not thinking straight. How could she even consider seeing him? It could only end in tears – her tears. Weren't her emotions turbulent enough without adding more to the mix? Louise needed a voice of reason. She reached for her phone and dialled Rae's number.

"Hey, you free for a coffee?" she asked.

"Sure," Rae answered. "Come on over. What's up?"

"Oh, you're gonna love this…"

"Oh god! I'm ready, whatever it is!"

Rae was one of those friends who could see the bigger picture. She was also Louise's confidante and knew her situation. Ten years Louise's junior, Rae had been eternally single, but enjoyed dalliances with long-term friends. Louise had been living a vicarious sex life by listening to Rae's tales of erotic escapades with her "boys".

Rae opened her door with a glass of wine in her hand. "I think this is more appropriate," she said, offering it to Louise with a grin. The two women walked through the hallway and settled at the kitchen table. After a few moments of sipping their wine in silence, Rae asked, "So, what am I going to love so much, Lou?"

Louise recounted the message exchange and couldn't help flushing just at the thought of Max. "I must be mad even considering this," she said.

"It's just a drink, what's the harm?"

"It won't be just a drink, Rae. You know the Max story, we don't do 'just a drink'."

"Okay then," Rae refilled their glasses before taking

Louise's hands across the table. "What exactly did you want to happen when you sent that text this morning? You weren't just texting to say hi. You had an agenda – much as you don't want to admit it. You have been horny for months; him at home is doing nothing to even acknowledge there's an issue. You texted Max for a reason. What was it?"

Louise leaned back in her chair and let out a long sigh. "I wanted someone to notice me. He was pleased to hear from me, he wants to see me."

"Okay, so what now? I know you want to see him."

Louise freed her hands from Rae's and ran her fingers through her hair, rubbing at the tension in her neck as she did so.

"Of course I want to see him. It's Max. But I'm married, for fuck's sake! It's not as easy as just hooking up, is it?"

"But it could be," Rae told her. "It could be just a one-off thing to give you some bloody relief! Louise, you have been miserable. You are too young not to be having sex. You are gorgeous, you're sexy, how him at home keeps his hands off you, I don't know. He won't talk to you about what's going on, and he won't listen to you. You deserve to have pleasure in your life, Lou."

Louise nodded, staring at her wine glass.

Rae continued, "I'm not advocating a full-on affair here, but you need something more than your vibrator. You know this man, you trust him."

"I do know him. Or I did, anyway. I don't know his situation at the moment, Rae, and I don't want to make a complete fool of myself."

"Go for a drink. Old friends catching up. You'll soon suss it out."

***

The following week, Louise was sitting in a bar in town, waiting for Max. It was midweek, which felt safer somehow, and she had gone straight from work. She had told her husband she was meeting a couple of friends from university for a catch-up. She was wearing a simple knee-length shift dress and sandals. She wore her hair long, the way she knew Max liked it. As she ran her finger around the rim of her whisky glass, she felt the breeze from the opening door and the unmistakable presence of Max. His hair was slightly longer, he was still unshaven, and he wore a black crew-necked jumper and jeans. Involuntarily, she gasped at the sight of him, and when his eyes found hers and he grinned, she smiled back broadly. Louise stood from her seat as Max joined her at the bar. He enveloped her in his arms and she instantly felt a familiar stirring in her abdomen. His scent had not changed and made her skin begin to tingle. His arms around her felt just as strong as they always had.

"Hey you," he said quietly in her ear, "you're a sight for sore eyes."

Once he released her from his embrace, Max waited to place their order while Louise found a table away from the main bar. She watched him standing there, drinking in the sight of this familiar man. She still wanted him.

He took a seat opposite her and handed her a fresh whisky on the rocks. She took a sip and gazed at him. He held her stare and smiled a devilish grin.

They chatted for a short while about work, then he asked if she was still married and seemed surprised when she said she was.

"Why that look?" she asked, laughing lightly.

"Well, I always figured you'd outgrow him," he replied with a shrug. "He never seemed to be enough for you."

There was a quiet moment before Louise had to ask, "And what about you? Are you seeing anyone?"

He shook his head as he put his glass down. "There was someone for a while. She just wasn't the one, y'know?" He looked at her then, no grinning now, just hunger. She felt her pulse quicken and the coil inside her begin to tighten. "Why did you text me, Lou? Why are you here?"

She took a deep breath to steady herself. Did she want to be upfront? Her fingers were fiddling with her glass, her nails tapping the rim. Part of her wanted to run away but, as they made eye contact again, there was only one thought on her mind: she wanted to fuck him.

Louise knew her skin was flushed and she licked her lips before speaking. "Honestly?"

"Honestly," he breathed, not dropping her gaze.

She let out a breath she didn't know she'd been holding and shifted in her seat. She could feel her heart pounding as she began to speak.

"Max," she spoke quietly, "I... I wanted to see you. Needed to see you."

He leaned toward her across the table and placed his hand over hers, gently stroking her wrist.

"Yes, but why?"

Her gaze dropped to their hands, her fingers now slowly tracing his. She looked up at him again, his eyes were dark, his lips slightly parted. She couldn't find the words. Instead, she stood from her seat, rounded the table and stood before him. He pushed his chair back and rose to standing, inches between them. She looked up into his face and drew her hand along his bristled jaw. His hand moved to her waist, tenderly stroking her hip.

"I need to feel you again," she whispered, the words almost catching in her throat.

"Are you sure this is what you want?" Max gently asked her.

"It's what I need."

The Camel's Saddle

BY AC ASQUITH

Content: religion, sexual exploration, penetration, fisting, oral sex, anal sex

When I touched you for the first time – and I mean You, touching the parts of you that the world doesn't normally see – it felt untrue. This could not possibly be happening. In the weeks we'd known each other, I'd leapt to various conclusions. Something about you seemed vegan. I expected tattoos underneath your medical scrubs. I thought hair would be in abundance. I was wrong on all counts, and I physically jumped at feeling naked skin beneath your underwear, with slickness down the centre of you, before sliding my finger along and around and in. You felt pure somehow, even though I knew then, and know more now, that you can be anything but. Inviting – that's the word. Shaved, you were more open than I expected. I could feel your wetness leaking out of you; could see it like slow teardrops.

I'd had a strange relationship with hair. Having previously lived as a practising Muslim for most of my adult life, I was used to the practice of 'fitrah', which includes hair removal. Men and women from the age of puberty, whether married or not, are required to remove their pubic and armpit hair at least once every forty days. It was something which had surprised me in the months after converting, when I overheard women in the mosque comparing methods of hair removal. I asked what they were talking about, and they were appalled that I didn't know. They were probably imagining what forestry was flourishing in my knickers. It may well be a revelation to know what's in the under-garments of any ostensibly Muslim person you meet. It is a pain, removing hair, having the itchiness of stubble, the annoyance of ingrown hairs. These days I wouldn't bother at all, except that you do and it seems unfair that I don't do the same, albeit just with a cheap supermarket trimmer rather than a sharp, wet blade.

The next time we met, we both knew it would be to fuck. I'd been at work all day and would catch myself thinking about it. I remember looking at myself in the bathroom mirror, thinking that hours later I would look different somehow, like the day after I lost my virginity as a 15-year-old and seemed to walk taller and wiser through the corridors at school. You'd promised me free rein, and that I could explore your body as I wished. Although I'd had nightclub fumbles with women in my student days, this was new. I think there was amusement in your eyes at how gleeful and excited I was, but it was contagious enthusiasm. You are non-binary, with a hard androgynous, masculine presence, but the prospect of having your chest and your cunt at my fingertips was electrifying.

Afterwards, I marvelled at how tasting you and feeling you were exactly as I'd imagined they would be. I told you

I'd had dreams over the years about having sex in this way, the sort of dreams which are so real you wake up believing it had all happened. Maybe it's because I knew my own body so well, that I knew our folds of flesh so well, the hard nubs of our clits, the smooth warmth of our juices. The different textures inside you were ones I had anticipated: muscular smoothness that squeezed around my fingers; the patch of rougher tissue on the upper surface which I could swear was swelling, and which I now know can be coaxed into making you squirt uncontrollably when you've been waiting a long time to come. The feel of you under my tongue made my heart race. Long slow licks from your arsehole to above your clit with the flat of my tongue; touching the tip of my tongue to your clit so lightly you could barely feel it; curling my tongue into your cunt to scoop up the liquid pooling there; sucking your clit into my mouth and letting my tongue swirl around you.

Oral sex is controversial in the Muslim community. Scholars are divided on its permissibility, with bizarre interpretations and edicts. Some will say it is allowed so long as the various secretions are not ingested, leading to a final decision on the spit versus swallow debate. But because scholars describe women as producing lubrication for the duration of sexual activity rather than a definitive endpoint (I think female ejaculation would blow many of their minds) this often led to a judgement declaring that oral sex to a woman was always impure. Which seems a little unfair, to say the least.

The first time you fisted me, I was bleeding. We'd already fucked on our periods. "It's just red blood cells," you said, and I tasted my metallic tang on your lips as we kissed. The blood was natural lube, and I'd always found coming was a cheap and effective analgesic for period pain. I was always horny as hell by the time I was about to bleed – although let's face it, with you I am always on fire – and you were happy to throw a towel on the bed and carry on. I remember being aware that you were adding fingers while you fucked me. I know what one feels like, and two, and three, but after that things got blurry and I reached down between my legs and could only feel your wrist, with your hand inside me up to the hilt, my skin stretched around you like a drum so I could hardly tell where I ended and you began. You were barely moving – I'm sure I couldn't have coped with the poundings I now beg you for – and I could feel everything, every muscle twitch from your fingers and my cunt, every millimetre your knuckles travelled inside me. I remember the way my clit felt – out of place somehow, or tightened in some way. I knew I wouldn't be able to come, but I loved the experience of being stretched, and made vulnerable, as if I were completely at your mercy. I knew I would want this again. I knew that in time I would be able to come with your fist inside me, and I do, and it makes me laugh with joy and it makes me cry with some deep and profound emotion that I can't even name yet. I ask you, "Can you feel me come? Can you feel me squeeze you?" Because although those orgasms travel in fizzing waves down to my toes and back, I can't feel my muscles contract when I am so full of you. "Yes," you said. "I can feel you. I can feel you."

Blood is anathema to sex in Islam. There's no penetrative sex while a woman is on her period, or postpartum – there are workarounds of course, but the scholars are again undecided, collectively, as to what's possible. One time I was feeling frustrated and argumentative at a women's study group at the mosque, and challenged the teacher about women's sexual pleasure whilst menstruating. "Masturbation isn't allowed ever. Penetrative sex isn't allowed while bleeding. What's to stop a husband pleasuring his wife with his hand?" I asked. There were confused looks. His hand? I continued, "After all, orgasms are natural pain relievers." The teacher's answer: "Why not just have a paracetamol?"

I can't remember who instigated butt play. I wish I could have bottled all of those firsts! Whoever it was, it was an unlocking and a kind of test. Is this okay? This is something I want, is it something you want? It must have been tentative to begin with – a passing over with a fingertip, or a lick that went lower than necessary – but the body cannot lie and our bodies want our truth. I particularly love laying you on your back and straddling your hips, facing away from you. You are pinned down and I can play with your clit, your cunt, your thighs, your arsehole. I move between them all just as I desire. Because of the angle, it confuses me as to whether I'm touching you or touching myself, and my movements are all as natural to me as when I learned to come as an adolescent. I'll have two fingers in your cunt and two in your arse. I'll tease your clit with a bullet vibrator while running small circles around the outside of your holes with my fingertips. I'll hold a buttplug inside you while you come so you can't push it out. I love making you wait. I love watching you twitch. On other occasions, I'll lie between your legs, and suck your clit while fucking your arse with a vibrator, or have you use the wand on yourself while I fuck both your holes with my fingers. The idea of having you filled is magical. I think you'd agree. I put my hand around your neck and feel for your pulse and squeeze and release, and the combination tips you over the edge and I watch for the way your neck moves and your left arm shakes and I know you're there. As for me, I love your strap inside me. Anal is especially good – that sharpness when you enter me, and then satisfaction – and I rub my clit, or you do, or you hold a vibrator against me while I build, and take it away, and tease me again, edging me until the sweat pours between my breasts and down the small of my back – which you tell me you love and I almost believe you. I will one day.

Anal sex is completely forbidden – haram – in Islam. Some rogue scholars will say it is permissible if it is just the tip of the penis, or if the wife agrees, but those scholars are few and far between. Yet for something so black and white, it is often asked about at meetings and conferences – usually via anonymous notes to the speakers – so I do wonder what is actually happening between the sheets in people's bedrooms. One time a woman approached me at the mosque and said she had a question about anatomy for me, as she knew I was a doctor. She was a PhD candidate in some obscure subject and was newly married. Yes, everything was alright; she wasn't unwell in any way, praise be to God. She just wanted to know exactly which hole should they be using for having sex? I had a rush of incredulity and sadness for her. We talked; she left, looking worried.

This is not to say that Islam is especially cruel or odd; we are all humans who live according to religious rulings, societal expectations, or personal histories which make little sense to one another. There are some minor victories in Islam for women along the way – such as sexual satisfaction being ideal for both parties, and that a woman can request a divorce if it doesn't occur – but the dice are loaded (not that gambling is allowed anyway!) in the favour of men. And, of course, only cis-het marriages would ever be legitimate, which is not the case for my partner and me, not that either of us is religious now. But there are some troubling traditions and rulings, which inevitably echoed into my sex life back then. Husbands can request sex at any time, and if a wife refuses without good reason and he is angered as a result, the angels will curse her until morning. Even if she is on her 'camel's saddle', she should not refuse. There is the spectre of polygyny – even though it's uncommon in the UK, Muslim men are still allowed to have up to four wives (through Islamic marriages, rather than civil). There are economic and social inequalities inherent within Islamic law which permeate the domestic relationship.

Which brings me to you, now, my love and my lover. I realise now what it is to desire and long for someone, and for someone to do the same, completely equally. I feel myself getting wet just thinking about you. I want my skin covered in your bite marks as possession. I want your spit in my mouth. I want you split open for me. I want your fingers twisting my nipples. I want your fist inside me. I want your hair in my grasp and your neck exposed for my teeth. I want your clit grinding on mine. I want my fingernails scratching down your back as I fuck you from behind. I want my hand around your throat. I want the sounds you make when you come. I want the juices you explode with when you squirt in gushing gasps. I want your strap down my throat until I gag and in my cunt until I twitch and in my arse until I come. The more I get, the more I want. I would jump off my camel's saddle for you in a heartbeat.

Sex is the Easy Part

BY TRINE LEHMANN HANSEN

Content: *exploring intimacy, redefining sex, Cuddle Club*

I am in the middle of a whole world of new experiences. I am filled with awe and wonder and wide-eyed curiosity. I am discovering intimacy.

In some ways, my sexual journey has been jumbled and turned upside down. I got curious about sex pretty early – but got started pretty late. I fell into the world of BDSM from the very beginning and didn't discover vanilla until a decade later, when I fell in love for the first time.

That ended in heartache and was followed by a 12-year-long dry spell, while I was single-mothering 24/7 and juggling stress and depression on the side.

A year and a half ago, I found renewed energy and that inspired me to join a dating site. A sex-dating site, in fact.

Even though I'm pretty hetero and cis, I have never believed that traditional relationships would be right for me. Or maybe it's because I never believed I was capable... (the jury is still out on that, but it's probably a bit of both).

For me, sex has always been the easy part while intimacy was difficult.

That made a sex-dating site the obvious choice for me. I wanted sex – not emotions and complications. So, I dived head first into a buffet of one-night stands.

It was great. I felt like I had a lot of catching up to do and a lot of things to explore, and I had certainly come to the right place for that!

Not only did I finally get laid again, but I also learned a lot about myself. I pushed many boundaries that were really just societal norms I had adopted. I grew a lot and my horizons expanded.

But it didn't take very long for it to start to feel a bit hollow. I came to think of it as fast-food sex. Just like I might sometimes crave and indulge in greasy fries and a scrumptious milkshake, it would leave me feeling a little bit yucky and unfulfilled after the 'rush' wore off.

Fast forward, past a long break, some inner turmoil and a lot of focus on other delicious aspects of life, and I arrived at a turning point.

On the sex-dating site, there was a wide range of events from social dining to fancy orgies. I signed up for a Cuddle Club event. It was fully clothed, safely guided, and in a lovingly held space. This was, and still is, the most scary and challenging thing I have done on my sex-dating journey.

I have come to realise, however, that when we do new things that we are genuinely ready for (even if we are not fully aware of this readiness), it can feel surprisingly natural and easy. This was one of those things.

The event was carefully and gently designed and it felt completely safe and natural to start with exercises designed to help us sense our boundaries. The hugs increased in duration and closeness until we ended up cuddling. By the end, I was completely intertwined with a total stranger for a full 15 minutes after a brief spooning.

I must admit, I was not completely unaffected by that final cuddle, and I felt a gentle electricity from him too. Neither of us crossed the boundary – sexual energy was allowed to be present but was not to be expressed.

After the event, I reached out to this man. I asked how he felt following the whole experience, and we started talking. I wanted to know if he would like to meet again – mostly to get to know each other now that we had already shared something so intimate and intense. We quickly and easily agreed that we would like to explore the hugs and cuddles a bit more too, all while staying within the 'boundaries' of the event.

I would be lying if I said I hadn't considered opening up to the possibility of letting the hugs and cuddles evolve. In a way, it was the obvious thing to do, and it would even have been the easy thing to do. Meeting for sex was familiar but inventing a cuddle date was uncharted territory.

Not opening the door that would inevitably lead to sex made this another big step for me. It was a curious experience to realise that I had total faith that I could trust that this man meant what he said and that our cuddle date wasn't a pretence for sex. I think we both felt a kind of reverence for the somewhat vulnerable experience we had shared, so I felt very safe exploring this strange new world with him.

We met at his place and there was just a very brief nervousness at first before the conversation found a delicious flow and openness. He was generous about sharing his thoughts and what had come up for him after the Cuddle Club event.

There is something very attractive about a man with

the ability and willingness to reflect so deeply and openly. Having grown up with the impression that men are useless when it comes to emotions, this was a very welcome addition to the evidence I have spent my life collecting to refute (what I now understand to be) my mom's beliefs.

It was also really nice that I got to be the one to initiate the next stage by saying, "Soooo... do you still want to cuddle?" Luckily he did! I have never really been good at being the one who takes the initiative, so having the opportunity to do it here was another gift.

We started with standing hugs – like we had done at the event. It was warm, gentle and very safe. There were no wandering hands or other attempts at nudging us towards anything more than what we had agreed to.

This felt very profound. Should it really feel like such a big deal that this man respected me, respected his own words, and respected our shared boundaries? (It's not the topic of this essay, but it's a question that lingers in my mind.)

Towards the end of our date, our closeness had centred on our necks and faces... We both got caught up in gentle nuzzles. Yet there were no kisses, as that was outside the scope of our date.

We ended up on the sofa, talking. His love language is touch, but mine is words, so we joked that sharing our thoughts like this was my aftercare – and it really felt that way. I have never needed aftercare, or maybe I just didn't even consider it to be an option, but here it was given so naturally and willingly.

During this talk, 'next time' came up. The nuzzling had surprised us both and we agreed that the skin-on-skin contact was special. So, we decided that next time would be more skin and therefore fewer clothes, but still all within the cuddle spirit.

The time between the first two dates was often filled with a soft electrical hum in my body. It was clearly a kind of turned-on-ness, but not the insisting kind that demands release.

When I sought that release anyway it was tricky because there was no fantasy associated with the turned-on-ness. It was not an '*I want to jump his bones*' kind of a turn-on, it was more of an '*OMG, I have met a person and found a space where I'm supported in exploring a new, vulnerable side, and I want more*'. But how do you get off on that?

There was so much to process, and I always do that best by writing out my thoughts. The dating site has a very active blog, where I have occasionally been sharing my thoughts and experiences throughout my journey. So, I wrote a blog post about my experience of the Cuddle Club and offered it to the facilitator to share as a testimonial.

Before that could happen, I knew I wanted to run it by my date first – since he was mentioned in the post. I emailed it to him and he surprised me again with his thoughtfulness, his attention to detail, and his reflectiveness. He sent back a reply that made me feel *seen* and *heard* to a degree I'm not even sure I have ever experienced before.

You can probably appreciate that I was looking forward to our second date!

When I got there, I tumbled through the door, my heart racing – which of course he noticed as we held each other close for our hello hug.

He admitted his own butterflies, which settled us nicely and easily into the conversation. He brought up a couple of details from my blog post and asked me to elaborate. That made any residual awkwardness evaporate instantly.

(When I told a friend about this she laughed and said, "If only men knew how easy we are – they just have to encourage us to talk about our thoughts and emotions.")

Our second cuddle date began with us sitting face to face. It turned into a cuddle as we moved closer and wrapped our legs around each other.

We had agreed that we wanted 'more skin and less clothes', but we had not defined what that meant exactly... I checked in with him: did he think that just meant shorter sleeves? Luckily, we agreed that it was a bit more than that.

My sweater soon became too hot, so off it went while we were still sitting in each other's embrace. He just held me. Caressed my back a bit, slowly and gently, but mostly we simply hugged. Then he asked if it was okay if he took off his shirt too.

Even on my way home from the first date, I knew that to me, 'less clothes' would ideally mean wearing underwear but being topless. I felt an urge not to hide my breasts; I wanted to let them be a natural and non-sexual part of me in this encounter.

I found the courage to ask if it was okay for me to be topless. His first instinct was to make sure it was not about me initiating sex or thinking that HE expected it. I assured him I just wanted less of a barrier between us. He thought about that for a moment and then offered to help me out of my bra.

It was SO nice just to sit there, chest to chest, arms and legs wrapped around each other. Just BEING. If anyone had told me it would feel so completely natural and unforced and easy, I wouldn't have believed them.

We talked and we sensed each other. He told me that he would like to follow up on the 'spoon' from the event and asked if I would be more comfortable on the sofa or if I wanted to move it to his bed. We chose his bed and got out of our jeans.

The spoon turned into caressing and gentle explorations. He trailed a few, subtle kisses up my neck and found my earlobe.

There was more face nuzzling, and we both felt the hint of a pull towards a kiss, but we let it pass and remained true to our shared intentions.

It was all so warm and sweet and soft and gentle. Only on my way home did I realise that my mind had been practically empty all that time. None of the usual thoughts running rampant – I had simply been present in my sheer delight and enjoyment of the moment.

But then, out of the blue, I was struck by tiredness and heaviness... It took me a little soul-searching to realise that the tiredness came from my thoughts about what 'more' meant for next time. There had been absolutely no pressure from him about what it meant, and I knew we felt very in sync about it, even though it was not fully defined.

I became aware that it had triggered a notion planted in my mind by a friend. She had recently shared with me how she sometimes suspected that her need for closeness caused her to trade sex for intimacy.

I never personally felt that way – at least not to a degree that made me consciously aware of it – but now I couldn't 'un-think' the thought, and it felt so wrong to bring that sentiment to our newly created space.

That night I was too tired to think coherently, so I sent him a text letting him know I had enjoyed the day, and that I would process and share my thoughts in the morning. Then I fell into bed at 10 p.m.. I awoke to a message from him: he was spending a night under the stars to process the day's 'body therapy' as he called it.

He was right: it WAS therapeutic. I thought of it as

'magical', but therapeutic or healing would actually be more accurate.

I sent him a long email with all my thoughts. I laid it all out there. I told him how amazed I was about what 'our project' was doing to me. I told him I felt very safe and comfortable letting him continue to explore my almost naked body. I told him I would like to add kisses if he was up for that too. And I told him I would like to take sex out of the equation.

Then I explained about the thought of trading sex for intimacy. I also made it very clear that this thought was coming from me and that I felt no pressure from him.

Opening the conversation about 'sex' meant I had to define it – since being almost naked together in his bed was cutting it a little close. Putting it into words helped me clarify my thoughts.

My list of sex that was off the table was penetration, oral, and orgasms.

Again, he blew my mind with his reply. He listened and acknowledged what I shared. He stood his ground by confirming that he did NOT want sex to be part of any kind of score-keeping or trade-off. He appreciated my openness and vulnerability. And he asked for clarification: the penetration and the oral part he understood and con-curred with. But he pointed out that orgasming would be my responsibility to stop if our 'non-sex' explorations got too intense. As he noted, orgasms can occur even without genital stimulation.

He had a point, and it set off even more thoughts for me about the definition of sex and why I felt that orgasms fell into that category.

This is still percolating in my system, but it's about a distinction between sensuality and sexuality – which, for me, ties in with 'bigger' thoughts and ideas.

I can connect this to the distinction between whether we focus on the journey or the destination in life. The last few years, after coming out of the other side of stress and depression, have very much been about me living and enjoying the journey.

I nearly killed myself chasing the outcome, the goal, the finish line, the destination. And somehow it has left me with an almost allergic reaction to any kind of pressure to achieve, and an aversion to chasing things.

And it seems that orgasms have been caught up in this. Maybe partly because of the very well-meaning men who were almost exhausting themselves while staring intensely at me, waiting for me to come.

While waking up this morning, and pondering the evolution of our meetings, I realised that the idea of feeling him inside me is more aligned and true to the intimacy and framework of the cuddle events than having a non-genital orgasm. So, somehow, penetration is less sex-ish than an orgasm...

I had to question that, and the answer that emerged was an image of how 'feeling him inside me' in itself could be a gentle, even 'still' experience of 'being' and connection, while an orgasm would somehow involve more 'doing', more chasing. It would feel like an outcome, a finish line, an achievement – trying to reach a destination.

I am not yet completely sure what to do with these realisations and insights, but I am pretty convinced there is more healing to be had – and more 'wholeness' – which was part of my motivation for joining the sex-dating site in the first place.

For most of my life, sex has felt like a separate aspect of me. Like it could not coincide with my daily life as a mom, daughter, friend, colleague, neighbour... Therefore, I decided to own my sex and dating journey, and to be open about it (without crossing anyone's boundaries about what they wanted to hear).

Integrating my sexuality into my overall personality has been therapeutic. Acknowledging myself as a sexual being has been highly liberating and empowering.

Now it seems like it's time to integrate intimacy into the mix as well. And I am so happy I have done the inner work that made me ready to meet a man who is so on board with creating this beautiful, safe space where we can explore and experience all the facets of intimacy together.

Unbreakable

BY MERRYN AUGUST

Content: bereavement, grief and loss, chronic pain, kink and BDSM, sexual identity

When my lover was dying, I kept telling myself, "It will be okay." Not in a 'she'll get better' way – I knew her illness was far too progressed for that – but in an 'I will survive' way.

I did survive. She did not. But, for a long time, I was left living a half-life.

We'd had a complicated relationship: long-term, long-distance, non-monogamous, and based on consensual, erotic, power dynamics. She wasn't just my lover and friend, she was also my Top, my Dominant, my fellow accomplice as I explored my submissive and masochistic side. In everyday life, we were both competent high-achievers. Alone, together, away from the rest of the world, I could stop trying to keep control of everything – including myself – and surrender. She needed sadism and masochism as much as I did and, fortunately, we were already hard-wired to converge from opposite polarities.

She was the only one strong enough to hold my power. I couldn't have given it to anyone else. I couldn't have trusted anyone else to know me in that way. Sometimes it was subtle (her teeth marks left around my nipples), other times it was more extreme (lying spreadeagled on the bed as her crop striped the backs of my thighs). She gave the orders; I willingly bent and stretched and knelt for her.

When she died, I was sure my submissive side had died too. I broke. Then I hardened. Now brittle, how could I dare risk inhabiting that space ever again? Surely, if I tried, I would shatter?

Years passed; sex happened. Her death had been like a wild bushfire to my sexuality: I was left ashen and devasted but somewhere, deep underground, seeds and roots had survived and, slowly, slowly, began to grow again.

Because I hadn't died, I decided that I owed it to her – and to myself – to live fully. If I'd been given more years than her, that meant I had to live for us both.

I attended a one-day workshop for people who wanted to connect with their pleasure and sexuality through 'conscious kink'. I needed a gentle and supportive way to get back in touch with this part of me. I also needed community – I'd been feeling very alone. Along with around twenty other intrepid explorers, I allowed myself to be guided by the facilitators as we explored a range of practices. In the morning, we connected to our bodies through 'anything goes' dance moves, and connected to our voices by shouting and screaming against a loud backdrop of heavy drumming. In the after-lunch session, we were told we'd be connecting to our power and how it felt to give and receive.

Lunch consumed, I returned (from being last in the loo queue) to find a room full of people standing in pairs. They'd started the session without me and I was left helplessly looking around for someone to stand beside. One of the facilitators came over to me. I knew she worked as a professional dominatrix and I was intimidated by both her job and her self-assurance. She smiled warmly at me, "You can work with me," she said and held up a blindfold.

The first practice was a warm-up trust exercise: the person giving their power was to wear the blindfold while the person receiving the power led them around the room, told them when and where to sit and stand, and so on.

I stood still while the blindfold was fastened at the back of my head. Behind the darkness, something immediately shifted in me and my grief rose, roaring to the surface. "I can't," I said, tears wetting the fabric covering my eyes.

"Do you want me to take it off?" she asked.

"No, I... I..."

"Here, sit down with me." She drew me onto the floor and cradled me between her thighs, holding me gently and quietly.

With everyone and everything else obscured, I finally managed to stammer through my tears, "She died. I had someone and she died."

At a play party some years later, I asked the same dominatrix to beat me. "I have to warn you," she told me, "I'm feeling particularly brutal tonight." She offered me the option of a blindfold and I gladly accepted it – I wanted to believe it was just her and me; I didn't need to witness what was about to happen to know it was real. I wanted her blows. I wanted to feel the edge of me soften a little. I had become so rigid on the outside: a necessarily sturdy container for the tumult of my emotions. I trusted that her brutality wouldn't be too much for me to handle and – equally – that my needs wouldn't be too much for her.

She expertly brought me from standing, arms braced

against a wall while she flogged me, to face down on the ground, my back and buttocks coloured and patterned by an array of implements. I felt every blow and, as each one landed, I remembered my courage, my resilience, and my strength. I remembered my Self.

She beat me until I called "red" – our agreed safeword to end play. I curled foetal on the floor, feeling equal relief that I'd been able to initiate the play *and* that it was now over. As I came down from the adrenaline and endorphin high, I found myself feeling numb and shell-shocked. I wasn't used to this kind of physicality without a deep emotional connection or any sexual release. But gradually, as days passed and my bruises turned from black to yellow, I began to thaw.

It was time, and I chose to allow the momentum of the meltwater to carry me towards another lover.

Their presence was like a lighthouse, a beacon in an otherwise churning sea. I sought them out for their solidity. Having lived with the ghost of memories for so long, I needed someone whose concreteness was unmissable. They could fill a concert hall with their presence and I knew they would be able to orchestrate and command symphonies from me – body and soul.

I found them because I was looking. Because I was open and ready. Because this part of me was determined to live.

Submission. Masochism. These are the places I go to feel most in my power. I feel potent, courageous, desired. I feel my strength and my ability to endure, and I take great pleasure in knowing that my surrender feeds my partner's needs as much as my own.

It turns me on like nothing else. My body lights up. My cunt swells. I take consensual pain and transmute it. In those moments, I am an alchemist, a magician, a witch.

A sacred whore. A witness to the fullness and wholeness of ourselves. Raw. Unfiltered. Released. It's an energy exchange where we both emerge as more than we were before. A vehicle for sexual and spiritual expansion.

Having been reunited with this part of me, it feels cruel to sense it being taken away again. More than that, the probability of impending loss feels frightening.

My body is changing in ways that are forcing me to look at my mortality. It can no longer move the way it used to (kneeling unsupported at the feet of my Dom is now painful in a bad, damaging, way). I live with unwanted and unpredictable chronic pain (planning anything – be it a weekend away with friends or a sexy dungeon scene – requires a leap of faith and a refundable deposit). I wistfully remember the days when I welcomed a slippery fist gradually entering me and how it felt like being held from the inside out (now I worry that anything too big or vigorous will lead to cystitis, tearing, and ongoing discomfort after sex).

This is the irony: where once I craved the physical, emotional, and transcendent sensations of consensual pain, now I fear the uninvited, everyday pain of living in a body that's breaking down.

And yet, I'm not ready to give up. My hard and fast fantasies have been replaced with pillows and props, extra lubricant, and a resigned acceptance that there are days (weeks, months) when I just can't "go there".

My lover says it is okay. They say it's enough to hold me, see me, smell me. But I know we both want more.

The new challenge is finding my strength and feeling my power in a different kind of vulnerability. The old me absorbed consensual pain. It nourished me. It was the spinach to my Popeye. I wore whip marks on my shoulders like a superhero's cape.

But now... Now there are days when I feel saturated with unwanted pain. So saturated that pleasure can no longer permeate me.

Is this true?

No.

Yes.

Sometimes.

I know what it's like to stand in the desert and feel my body desiccate into a million fragments. I know what it's like to feel that first drop of rain on parched skin, to drink it in, and feel something begin to grow again. I know what it's like to hope and want and search and find. And I know what it's like to lose.

I also know what it's like to remember who I truly am. On those occasions when I am able to play, I register my lover's caresses – the tender and the ferocious – and my body remembers. Oh, how it remembers! *I remember this pleasure,* my body gasps. *I remember being so focused on the moment that I forget to worry about the future. I remember the euphoric joy that arises from intense connection.*

I've recently discovered that taking part in consensual pain play can feel like hitting the reset button on my pain receptors. For a glorious 24 hours afterwards, I'm floating on air. I'm free. Untethered. Unbroken once again.

Which has led me to wonder: what if this isn't the end but simply a new iteration?

My first Top helped me to open a doorway into a world where my fantasies were welcomed and reciprocated. I learned how to ask, and how to receive.

With my new Dominant, I've discovered how to relinquish more control. And how to give even more of me: more of my attention, more of my vulnerability, more of my honesty.

There's always a growth edge.

Perhaps these are simply growing pains?

Perhaps this life stage is about letting go even more. Letting go of expectations and, instead, giving my focus to what is. Because 'what is' is a body that felt a jolt of lust when my lover left me a voice note during their working day. The resonance of their voice vibrated within me at a frequency stronger than any of my discomforts. 'What is' is my lubed-up fingers on my clit, coaxing my orgasm to the surface. A reminder that pleasure is always within my reach and heals me in the deepest of ways. 'What is' is exploring new fantasies – in my head as well as in my bed. Because I'm not the person I was thirty years ago and my sexual self doesn't need to stay chained to the past.

This is what is. Today. Now. A choice I make every day not to forsake myself. My submission. My masochism. A decision and a commitment to reframe pleasure, intimacy, and desire as many times as necessary to keep them present in my life.

Earth-animal

BY BRITT FOSTER

Content: beyond gender, beyond the physical, intentional celibacy

The formless essence of me sloshes between 'man' and 'woman', unable to fill either shape with a sense of identity. I am creature. Earth-animal. An event of ceaseless transformation.

When I was twelve years old, a psychic divined that my consciousness was floating above my body instead of anchored inside it, and I'd never felt more seen. This body is creature. Earth-animal. I watch from a metre above her warm flesh, a metre above the heart and its blood and the brain and the skeleton. I watch, and yet I am. Her eyes are mine to see with. Her fingers are mine to type. I have become the vessel, I have always been the vessel, and maybe it's true that the brain dreams the separation.

The formless essence of me cannot grasp concepts like masculine and feminine. I am drawn to anything that strays from what mainstream programming tells me those concepts mean. I am drawn to the people who rake their fingers through the shape of those words; break them into fragments that ripple in distorted inversions.

When I was twenty-four, I used sex to embody myself. I imagined this body full of me. Brimming with soul. I've always wanted to understand what 'woman' meant. 'Girl'. These words were used to describe me from the moment I came screaming into the oxygen, swaddled in a pink blanket and given the name 'Brittany'.

I wanted to understand women, so I loved them. And I fucked them. And they made me pant and sigh and laugh and scream in ecstasy.

I grew up and I was a girl, but no one could ever tell me what 'girl' really meant. No one could tell me what 'boy' really meant, either. They tried, but

(it's not pink and blue and dresses and trousers and long hair and short hair and makeup and heels and cooking and cleaning and babies and gender is a social construct it's a performance and I sucked when I played the moon in my 4th-grade classroom rendition of *A Midsummer Night's Dream*, I sucked at being the moon but I made an impressive lion mask –)

the formless essence of me knows

I am creature. I am beast and tree and crawling insect. Energy ebbing and flowing and concentrated a metre over this body. Her body. Their body. My body.

On a subatomic level, we are energy in motion. My body contains pieces of all the people who have touched it. I often imagine what it looks like; a fine mist exchanging its particles. Sex speeds up the process. Hands are change makers. When her hands reach inside me, or I reach inside of her, we give and take and change irreversibly.

Years later, when she's gone, I still find myself speaking through fragments of her personality.

The formless essence of me contains the formless essence of others. There is 'man' and 'woman' and what it means to those who feel those words inside themselves, and there is 'neither' and 'both' and 'everything' and what it means to those who feel the absence of those words. My identity still fluctuates.

I am soul. I am the observer. I am motion.

When I was twenty-seven, and then again at thirty, I took a year of intentional celibacy to find the self amongst all the pieces of others. I shut the gates of my body, took a broom and started sweeping. I stuffed trash bags full of interference, purged all the energy that wasn't my natural colour. I visualised myself cutting the cords again and again and again. But

I still find myself speaking with fragments of their personalities.

I taste the shape of my smile on some days and think: "This belongs to her; I know exactly what it's like inside the smile she used to give me."

I fucked women, I fucked men, I fucked the grey space in between, and I still cannot fill the shapes of gender with identity. I've never felt completely human. I've never felt 'woman'. I don't want to play the moon or learn the script for my performance. I won't put colour on my lips to conform for the limelight.

I am Earth-animal.

I draw lion masks.

Our Capacity for Passion:
Seasons of Sensuality

BY MARIA CYNDI

Content: childhood sexual abuse, medical intervention, disability discrimination, evolution of desire

As a woman, I am objectified by society, but silenced. As a disabled person, I am desexualised by society, but silenced. As a MeToo survivor, I have been shamed by society, but silenced. It is now *my* time to speak *my* truth.

My relationship with my body has always been complicated. Being born paraplegic in an ableist and often hostile society, taught me from a very young age, that I was different, and that *difference* made me ugly. Add painful, invasive medical intervention and years of molestation into the mix and it's no surprise that by the time I reached adulthood, I had gone through enough trauma to shut me down completely.

It has taken the whole of my adulthood to recover from my childhood and, at times, the healing process has felt too much for me. I've had years of therapy and needed every moment of every session to process the horrors I've witnessed and had gaslit by the very people who should have been my refuge.

As I came to the end of my teens and watched my non-disabled peers fall in love for the first time (some moved in together, some got engaged, some even got married), I began to realise that if I was to have any hope of a future healthy relationship, I would need to undo some of the damage first. At the age of twenty, I chose to have sex with two men (not at the same time). These sexual encounters were not relationships and both men were aware that they were under no obligation to buy me flowers.

The first guy was quite a bit older than me. He was twenty-six. He was mature, quiet, and sensitive. I had known him as a friend for just over a year and he knew why I wanted to have a 'no strings attached' evening with him. On the night we chose to get together, I went to his flat and we had a few drinks, I guess for Dutch courage. I remember I was shaking as I held my glass of Tia Maria, which I think I gulped down in one go. He took my empty glass from me and placed it on the lampstand at the side of the couch. As he turned back to face me, he put his arm around me, tenderly kissed my cheek and grinned. He kissed me gently, but passionately. As our lips parted, he gave me a cheeky smile, which seemed to calm me. We kissed again, this time deeply. My feeling of fear started to change into a feeling I hadn't had before. My nipples were hard and tingly and I kinda liked it! I remember we both took our own clothes off. He was very patient with me as I nervously took my time. As we lay down, he positioned himself between my thighs, holding himself up and away from my body, allowing me to choose when our belly buttons touched. He was so gentle with me and kept asking if I felt okay. After kissing and cuddling for a while, I could feel his penis stiffen and move up across my stomach. He reached for a condom and kissed me again. I felt him slide inside me and, in that moment,

I shut my eyes tight and froze. He stopped and whispered, "Open your eyes, please... It's okay, I'm not going to hurt you... Go on, look at me." I opened my eyes to see a kind, gentle face looking back at me. We kissed and continued to move together until he gasped, and everything stopped. I didn't orgasm... but I also didn't die either, so I was happy.

A few months later, we met for a drink and I went back to his flat once more. This time felt familiar and I wasn't so nervous. We slowly undressed each other – which felt very powerful to me. This time, I didn't shut my eyes tight with fear. This time, I wanted to remember everything. I wanted to see everything. It might sound silly, but from keeping my eyes shut tight as a child whilst being molested, and not having sex education at the special school I attended – because it was assumed disabled children wouldn't need to know about sex as nobody would want to have a relationship with us in the future – I didn't have a clear idea how a penis or testicles were attached to the body.

He allowed me to take my time to learn how all his bits and pieces fit together. I lay down beside him as we held each other and kissed. Just like the first time, the moment was over without me having an orgasm, but it was pleasurable. I stayed for a cup of tea and then went home. I saw him socially a few times after that but our lives changed and we eventually lost touch.

The second guy I chose to have sex with was nearer my age, at least on paper. I think emotionally, he was much younger. I didn't tell him why I wanted to sleep with him, and I don't think he cared. He was just happy to get his leg over with someone he didn't need to call the next day. He was a fun, free-spirited man-boy, he liked to party hard, drink a lot and smoke weed. He was like a firework in human form and his energy was intoxicating. I slept with him twice. With him, I was still very inexperienced but more in control of how I wanted things to go. I had a clearer idea of what I wanted from the experience, and I felt more confident. Having sex with him felt more organic, natural and less like sex therapy. Again, it was over without me experiencing orgasm, but by the end of that year, I was a changed woman.

My twenties were about finding myself and, subsequently, finding my life partner. Most of my non-disabled peers had moved away so I had to rebuild my social life from scratch. I joined several groups and clubs and, in doing so, met a lot of interesting people.

After having consensual, loveless sex with two guys, I went on to date a blind guy. We were together for a couple of months and parted amicably. During my time with him, my self-confidence grew beyond my wildest dreams, and I will forever be grateful to him for giving me the confidence to continue to grow as a human and keep pushing back when the world tries to push me away. His inability to see me meant he was attracted to my voice and personality. In a world that made me feel ugly and undesirable as a disabled woman, *his* disability liberated *mine*.

Not long after this relationship ended, I was invited to a 21st birthday party of an old friend I'd known my whole life. I agreed to go and I'm very glad that I did because I met the most beautiful soul I've ever known – my future husband. THIS was the guy I had healed for. THIS was the relationship that was going to continue to nourish and soothe me for the rest of my life.

Six months into our relationship, I moved into a fully accessible ground-floor flat and embarked on an independent life as a paraplegic woman. Another six months later, the love of my life moved in with me. In truth, we could've moved in together straight away, but I desperately needed space to grow, and I wanted to know that I could manage on my own if we split up. We're both quiet, shy and easy-going, so conflicts were few and far between and usually caused by external stressors, like university deadlines and work commitments, rather than a clash of personalities. Once I had my own space at the flat, our intimacy escalated quickly. It was during these hedonistic first few months of freedom, that we discovered the convenience of me sitting in a comfortable position in a wheelchair whilst enjoying fellatio, without the unnecessary discomfort of kneeling on a hard floor and getting pins and needles in my toes.

We lasted just over a week of sharing a bed before we had sex. Our first time together was a mixture of sexual energy and nervousness, for both of us. This wasn't my first sexual encounter, but it *was* the first time it mattered. I wanted the experience to be perfect, or at least perfectly imperfect. We were so young and naive, we fumbled and bumbled our way out of our clothes and lay down on the living room floor, in front of the fire.

With the TV on in the background to muffle the sounds of bodily fluids sloshing and our vocal expressions, the moment was passionate, tender and messy! We loved, we hugged, and we giggled our innocent way through the night, until we eventually decided to go to bed – to sleep. I didn't orgasm that night either and was beginning to wonder if I was sexually defective. It was many years later before I understood why my body was so reluctant to let go and surrender to the moment. It was tied to the abuse I had survived as a child. Thankfully, the man I fell in love with, the man who fell in love with me, was willing to patiently and lovingly help me, and bring me to a place where I could eventually be completely in the moment and more importantly, be in my body, not my head.

We lived like this for two years. Some friends of ours got engaged, so we bought them The Karma Sutra on video, which, of course, we had to watch before we wrapped it, in case it was 'faulty'... There weren't many positions I couldn't manage which, given my physical limitations, was quite impressive. We became more adventurous and even had sex in the shower a few times, although, on one occasion, we did stumble to the floor (undeterred, we continued to sex-surf across the soapy, wet bathroom floor until we ended up under the sink on the other side of the room, where I banged my head on the basin).

We got engaged the year after our friends. It wasn't a surprise engagement. We'd had many conversations about the future and if my physical limitations were something he really wanted to live with, long-term. Romance is one thing, but a legally binding contractual agreement to love each other, for better and for worse, for richer and poorer, in sickness and in health, is something else entirely. I'm very glad we didn't fall headlong into the romance of a fairytale marriage, because two days after we got engaged, I was involved in a road traffic accident that has subsequently, altered the rest of our lives.

Sex was put on the back burner for about eighteen months while I got through the worst of my injuries and weekly physiotherapy. I was still young enough to bounce back to a point where I regained most of my independence, but I've had chronic pain ever since. During this time, we were also going through the process of finding out if I could get pregnant. The thought of making a family and spending the rest of my life with the man I loved more than anyone, kept me going when the pain was awful. Once we were given the green light from the doctors to have unprotected sex and see what happened, we had LOTS of sex!

My thirties were a huge adventure into marriage and parenthood. We had our first baby the same year we got married. At a time when we perhaps should've been having more sex than ever, we were changing nappies and tackling night feeds.

A vital piece of information nobody passes down the generations in parenthood is that the very thing that makes a baby happen, gets completely thrown out of the window the moment you have one. We were so tired, we could barely make coherent conversation, let alone make love. Sleep deprivation is a very effective contraception. The dynamic of our relationship naturally changed with the addition of a new member of the family. My husband went to work every day and I was a stay-at-home mum.

Although we loved each other deeply and had the life we had chosen to create for ourselves, our individual roles as breadwinner and homemaker did give us very different experiences of family life, and this difference was reflected in the bedroom. By the time we got to bed each night, we were both completely spent and had no desire for anything. There must have been a shift in our energy at some point because when our son was two and a half, we had a second baby. She completed our beautiful family and life was blissful... apart from our capacity for passion. She didn't sleep through the night until she was three years old and by that time neither my husband nor I could hardly remember our own names.

I was very sick during my second pregnancy and for the first twelve months of my daughter's life, I couldn't sit up for more than one hour in every five. It took three years to heal completely, which also had a negative impact on our sex life. Our relationship was held together by the joint project of parenting and without realising it, we started calling each other 'mum' and 'dad' when we spoke to each other.

We weren't unhappy... just changed. We had become something different. The focus was no longer solely on us and *our* needs. We had to be available for our children, one of whom is disabled and has additional needs. On reflection, this decade was the most challenging of our whole relationship and there were times when we thought we wouldn't make it through the rough patches... but we *did*. The challenges we faced forced us to mature, communicate better, and listen with an open mind and heart. To hear each other and have patience with each other's emotional limitations under pressure.

Intimacy isn't just about inserting body parts into each other. We became closer during this decade, just by having the tenacity not to give up on each other. We learned the true meaning of love, not just the feeling of electricity flowing through our bodies when we were naked, and I think, ultimately, the lessons we learned made us better lovers. We started out meek, timid and in love. The challenges of parenthood made us feisty. We argued more and had to develop the skills to stand our ground when we believed we were right, and the humility to back down when we knew we were wrong.

We became very skilled at making lemonade out of lemons and rising from the fire like two, very determined, horny phoenixes! When we did have sex, it was very passionate, largely because opportunities were few and far between so there was a lot of sexual tension built up. It was during this time in our relationship, that I started to have orgasms more frequently.

It's difficult to have sex with children around. It's

difficult to find the energy, the time and the space... and trying to coordinate all three is like going on a mission that would make Indiana Jones quake in his boots. I remember one Saturday morning; we had woken refreshed from a relatively good night's sleep for parents of two toddlers. We snuggled into each other, and this evolved into kissing, which evolved further into caressing until we were actually making love... It was nothing short of miraculous.

Just when I thought life couldn't get any better, I noticed a small person standing in the doorway of our bedroom, quietly watching as daddy was riding mummy, like a horse. We didn't stop (I'm not sure we could) we simply lay down flatter under the duvet and carried on. By the time we were finished, the small, innocent figure had gone back into their bedroom. During breakfast, we talked about how much mummy and daddy loved each other and that sometimes we liked to have special cuddles that were just for grown-ups. Neither of our children seemed traumatised by the event and from that point forward we decided, as parents, to be open and honest about anything and everything. If they had a question, we had an answer.

My childhood had been a toxic mixture of not being given any information about intimacy yet, ultimately being over-exposed to the horrors of paedophilia because nobody protected me. I was determined that my children were going to learn about pleasure, passion, desire, love, tenderness and consent.

As my thirties neared their end, I noticed my hormones surging. I was hornier than I had been in my entire life, and I think my husband was becoming quite intimidated. It was during this time that I started to masturbate. I realise that is quite late, but I had been conditioned to believe that the lower half of my body was just for decoration and touching myself hadn't even crossed my mind. However, I was completely wired and had to do something. My nipples were becoming hard and enlarged at random times of the day and ached for attention. The most effective relief I got was from keeping a couple of teaspoons in the fridge and placing them inside my bra. I don't know if anyone else has tried this... but I highly recommend it.

Motherhood had been a challenge. Not because my children were difficult; they were dream children and a pleasure to be around, in fact, I missed them when they went to bed. It was difficult because of the cynicism and scepticism from everyone I met about my ability – as a wheelchair user – to parent them. I felt constantly under pressure to prove my worth as a parent and knew I had to be twice as good as everyone else to get half the recognition. This took its toll on me emotionally and physically. I was exhausted and so stressed I weighed just 29kg.

As a couple, we were so focused on raising our children and meeting *their* needs every day, that we didn't stop to consider how to meet each other's, or our own. In fact, I'm not sure we actually knew what our needs were at that point.

My forties were a curveball we didn't see coming. Desperately trying to just get from one end of each day to the other, in as few pieces as possible, there was no time for self-reflection. Until one morning I rolled over in bed and felt something rip in my shoulder, followed by searing pain, then complete numbness in my arm. This was the start of a very, very long road back to normalcy... and the beginning of the end of our sex life.

Three surgeries in four years plus the time it took to recover from said surgeries as a paraplegic (completely reliant on my upper body to do absolutely everything for myself) I consequently had to surrender what little independence I had as a disabled woman. It was losing my independence that made me feel truly disabled for the first time in my life. I had always been a wheelchair user and my life skills were learned within the context of that reality, but this newfound limitation destroyed my sense of who I was in the family dynamic, as I was completely unable to contribute anything useful as a mother or wife. My husband had to leave his job and become my full-time carer, which not only drained our finances but also robbed him of *his* independence too.

I was prescribed tramadol, amitriptyline, gabapentin and morphine during these ten years of hell, but all they did was incapacitate me more. The realisation that I have chronic pain and will live like this for the rest of my life has been devastating for both of us. Thankfully, I have managed to wean myself off all the medication as the side effects were a nightmare, but I am left with constant pain that nobody is aware of. Pain is something we can all understand and relate to, but our own pain is a very lonely experience.

During these first four years of my forties, we didn't have sex at all. Not once.

By the time I was forty-seven, the perimenopause had taken hold. My body shape and weight had changed to the point where I no longer recognised the woman with desperation in her eyes staring back at me in the mirror. I'd had body dysmorphia most of my life (which is no surprise) but adjusting to this rapid change in who I am as a woman, has been, and continues to be, extremely complex. It's so very difficult to feel connected to your partner when you no longer feel connected to yourself.

After the electric surge in my sex drive during my thirties, this was a dramatic change in our relationship. Sexually, we had drifted apart. Neither one of us even mentioned sex... for six years.

During this time, our children were going through the greatest challenges of their education, personal growth and development, so we did what we had done many times before, we found our connection through co-parenting.

GCSEs, A levels and a Diploma led to them applying to university. In September 2020, during the early stages of the global COVID-19 pandemic, both our children moved out of our family home and into university halls. I didn't experience the empty nest everyone had been warning us about. What I actually felt was relief. Not because I was glad to see the back of my babies, but because I no longer felt like I was under a spotlight. The pressure to carry out every aspect of motherhood to a faultless, unrealistic standard, at all times, no matter what the cost to my physical or mental wellbeing, had been unbearable. I didn't realise how stressed I'd been for two decades until it stopped.

Our house was eerily quiet, and we didn't really know what to do with our free time for a while. Sex wasn't even on my radar as an option. I had become sensually dead, to be honest. I didn't miss intimacy. I didn't even think about it until my husband made gentle advances, which were met with awkward apologies as I pulled away. I felt very guilty about my lack of pizzazz in the bedroom, but I genuinely had nothing.

We eventually settled into sharing our hobbies. Each evening after dinner, I would set up my whittling box of tricks, where I made chess pieces. (I love everything about playing chess.) My husband sat just beside the dining table where I was chipping away at blocks of wood. His hobby is computer programming. We chatted and laughed as we each enjoyed our hobbies and time together, learning to connect with each other in a meaningful, but non-sexual way.

Passion, lust, pleasure, orgasm and desire are all fundamental aspects of a sexual relationship and I believe they are vital to overall physical, mental and sexual health, but when the pilot light goes out on your libido, you have to redefine intimacy. I think we did this remarkably well and, moreover, we have survived!

My fifties have, so far, been a sexual revolution. It started rather abruptly with a slight panic as my husband was about to show me a photograph on his phone, but as he was scrolling, his finger slipped and the image that was left on the screen was of a naked woman. I knew by the fact that I could see her ribs, that it was definitely not me (I haven't seen my ribs for twenty years!). I also knew that we were not having sex. My heart sank. I asked him outright who she was and if he was having an affair. I will never forget the look of horror on his face as he knelt beside my wheelchair and wrapped his arms around me, assuring me that I was the only woman on the planet that he wanted to do naughty things with. He explained to me that whilst he fully understood that the perimenopause had robbed me of my desires, *his* were still in full force and he used this photograph as a visual aid during masturbation.

Whilst this was a rather traumatic half-hour, it did force us to address the elephant in the room. The fact that it had been ten years since we'd had full intercourse. We talked about the passage of time and how it had taken its toll on each of our bodies. We talked about how I had been let down by doctors who, because they saw a woman in a wheelchair, hadn't considered the possibility that I might have enjoyed sex with the man I love and that, *actually*, the fact that my libido was now like wet cardboard, *did* matter and needed fixing.

This conversation ended up being a deeply healing experience for both of us. We both talked about things we had kept to ourselves for years. We shared the reality of how much we genuinely loved each other and, despite my lack of sex drive, how much we still fancied the pants off each other.

Over the course of a couple of months, I sought peri-menopause support from a private clinic, and we moved to a new GP practice. Once that was established, I started taking HRT. One of the main problems I was having in perimenopause was how dry and irritated my body had become, both inside and out, from my hair to my mouth, my skin, eyes, vulva and vagina. While we waited for the HRT to start having a positive effect, we decided to try simply cuddling in the shower. As we soaped each other down, the wet, slippiness of the soapy bubbles felt amazing on my body. As our hands continued to explore parts of each other we had long lost and forgotten, I felt his hand slide between my thighs and his fingers between my labia. I began to massage soapy froth around his pubic hair, penis and scrotum as we passionately kissed. This is what we'd been missing. We just needed moisture and a little confidence to get over the mental barrier of fear it would be uncomfortable. It wasn't uncomfortable at all. It was amazing. I continued to massage his penis until it became hard, then rinsed the soap away and slid it into my mouth. Rhythmically in sync with each other, he thrust his fingers gently back and forth, in and out of my vulva and vagina as I rocked back and forth, intermittently taking as much of his shaft into my mouth as I could, then playfully licking the tip and frenulum, until we both orgasmed. You see, non-disabled people think of me as a burden and consider my husband as someone to be pitied, but in truth, *our* truth, we meet each other's needs perfectly. I do need help in the shower. But so does he...

This was the beginning of our second honeymoon. We powerfully took back our sex life and I powerfully took back my pleasure experience. We continue to have an incredible sex life, making love several times a week, and I have had the most mind-blowing, life-altering orgasms of my entire adulthood. We understand each other now, we understand each other's needs. We're in our fifties and no longer shy, at least with each other. We can openly communicate our sexual needs, without judgement. There's wisdom in our sex life now. It's not just physical. It's not just sensory. It's a deep understanding of each other and our desires. We have never really been able to be spontaneous with our sex life, there are too many considerations to account for when becoming intimate as a disabled person with chronic pain. Energy levels, pain management, the need for painkillers beforehand, pillows, cushions and a sex wedge to ease our joints (we're never quite sure if the creaking is coming from the bed or our ageing bodies), but there's a romantic truth in planning intimacy. A promise to each other. A commitment, that we will dedicate quality time to each other and our passionate desires.

We're learning more about each other now than we have during all the years we've shared, combined. Our children are settled in their new-found independence and no longer need us in the ways that they used to, and this has freed us up to focus on ourselves and each other. Naked Thursdays are back on and if we want to, we can make passionate love on the dining table, all night long.

Relationships are not meant to be pain-free and perfect. Life is complicated and humans are complex organisms. If we try to live up to the unrealistic expectations of a fairytale or social media, we will inevitably fail at everything. Being human means being messy. There is no secret to a successful relationship. We love each other, but more importantly, we like each other. The only thing that can come between us is the lack of desire to be together.

Let the Joy In

BY KAAN K

Content: *gender identity and intimacy, futuristic setting, oral sex, penetration, genital surgery*

Red checked the street one last time before they rang the buzzer. There was a sharp bang as the doorbot yanked open a shutter and gave Red a once-over. It was a silly thing; with a glossy pink and red shell. Humanoid, with all the expected limbs, except a head that was shaped like a pair of lips with two ridiculously googly eyes resembling the flame heart emojis.

"Password?"

"473113."

The bot opened the door and handed Red a robe and towel as they entered.

"I see you've been before?" it asked. Red nodded. "Would you care to fill out a quick feedback form about your experience at the centre? Your feedback helps us improve our services for your future enjoyment."

"I'm okay thanks. Can I go upstairs?"

"Most certainly, Red."

Red made their way down the dark corridor plastered with pictures of old porno pages. Although the centre had long been a place that catered to gay men, and had recently started inviting in other queer people and targeting their advertising at trans folk, the marketing team clearly hadn't thought to update their entrance décor. This corridor in particular made Red feel like they had entered a gentleman's club, and it set them slightly on edge. It reminded Red of what felt simultaneously very present and like another life all at once; when they used to dance in places with a similar vibe. Some of the customers had been alright, but there was more than one man who made Red shudder with discomfort just at their memory.

As they wandered down the corridor, they consciously took in a breath and tried to relax their shoulders. They could already hear the moans up ahead. The breathy "oohs" and gentle sighs and a person with a deep, loud voice begging to be fucked deeper. They passed rooms of people playing. Some with doors closed, others open. They caught glimpses of tongues intertwined and thighs over shoulders. There was a group of people smoking outside the lift and they shuffled to one side as Red approached. A cute person in a crimson corset made eyes at Red as their lips closed around their rollie.

"Hey babe," they greeted. Red nodded shyly in response but slipped past and the lift doors shuddered shut behind them.

The third floor was better lit than the ones beneath it; with a wider lilac corridor lined with deep purple velvet sofas. Red wandered along until they found a free room, then changed the sign on the door to 'occupied' before slipping in and locking the door behind them. The room was small, with a single lamp in the corner and a bright, jarring overhead light that Red immediately flicked off. There was a velvet armchair against one wall, a bed against the other, a small table, and a computer in the corner. They made their way towards the monitor and typed in their access code.

Welcome, Red! flashed up on the screen, alongside some cute drawings of tits and dildos by a queer illustrator they liked. They could customise this part and had spent most of their first visit doing just that. They'd been a nervous wreck, truth be told. They had come in, made all these personalisations to their avatar and user experience, and then left without doing anything else. This was their third visit.

Red had always been laughed at for being old-school amongst their friends, for not trying new things or flowing with change. The dating app boom thirty years ago had given rise to a new way to hook up: sex clubs like these where you could have a first meeting with someone, or multiple people, you'd met online. They were basically horny hotel rooms – you paid a monthly membership fee or a small fee per hour to have access to beds, sofas, playrooms and a space to hook up without judgement and on neutral ground. Each person stated their desires and the app would match them with people who had similar wants. Then you would chat with those people about requests, boundaries, what got you hot etc. If you got on well enough, you could arrange to meet here to play out a fantasy with the other person.

Red's heartbeat knocked up against the back of their throat. They squinted at the computer, clicking through the questionnaire that had been chosen by the algorithm and reflected Red's desires back at them. It asked them what they were in the mood for today, and Red tried to relax into it, as if this whole situation wasn't weird as fuck. As if they hadn't basically been prescribed this place by a doctor who'd recommended it for test-driving their new dick, something they'd dreamed of for a long time, but were pretty unsure of now it was here.

They closed their eyes and remembered Flip. Her thighs tight around their waist as she held their head against her tits and looked deep into their eyes.

"God, you fuck me well," she'd told them more than once. "I love your cock. You know how to fuck me better than any man ever did."

After they made her come hard, Red would slip off their strap and they'd fall asleep wrapped up in each other's arms. Cosy. Or sometimes Red would keep their dick on overnight, and the next morning Flip would rub it gently over the top of their pyjama bottoms and they'd both get turned on at the sight of Red's bulge and what it might make them both feel next.

That was more than five years ago now. And if Red was honest, they hadn't let anyone love them like that since. In the hospital room, after their surgery, they'd woken up with this thing between their legs and they felt... not much really. It came with a user instruction manual that they read feverishly over the next two weeks as they recovered in bed. It was an unglamorous healing journey, with friends coming over to help them eat food and piss, so stark from the sexy daydreams they'd had.

After four weeks, it was healed enough that they could take it off and on again. There were two types of surgery: one where the cock was permanent and another where it was detachable. Red had opted for detachable because their transness was ever-shifting and changing, and they liked the option of having a cock and a cunt. It was amazing to think that even ten years ago this kind of surgery didn't exist and trans people were still having to fundraise phenomenal amounts to get things like top surgery where they couldn't even feel their nipples afterwards. Since the last government was overthrown fifteen years ago, technology had moved fast for trans people, and all sorts of marginalised folk. Now that no one was forced to work to survive, many chose to pursue creative and research projects. Scientific discovery was far more independent than it ever had been, and most neighbourhoods had bustling community science labs. With this came space for trans people to develop better solutions for their bodies. Even some of Red's mates were involved in the tech advances that led to them having the kind of body they had dreamed of. A cock that not only was detachable but functioned so perfectly when it was there. It was grown in a lab from their own cells; it had their soft skin, their pubic hairs, it was thick and got alert and hard when they were turned on. So why could they not get it to cooperate?

The doctor (a very small and soft trans boy with a wispy beard and a baritone voice) had advised them to give it some time. He'd had a similar surgery, though in earlier days when the procedure wasn't as perfected, and it had taken him time too. He advised Red to try their cock out themself, or in judgement-free spaces with others, to build their confidence. It had been six months since the surgery and Red had experienced the occasional good wank, but most of the time their dick just felt like something they didn't really know what they were doing with. And it was more than that; they felt ashamed. They weren't sure who would want them for their transness or their altered body. Could they call themself a dyke any more? Would the gay boys be interested or see them as some half-formed thing? Would they ever be right for someone – not just acceptable, but have the kind of body others craved and fantasised about as they touched themselves?

Red selected some pretty trad lesbian porn on the computer. Like everything, it had a huge banner underneath it that said *Are you ready?* and a flashing button with the word *Yes* that you could click any time.

As the scene between the women escalated, Red felt their cock tingling and looked down. They ran their hand over the top of their jeans and traced its outline. Over the next few minutes, they felt it slowly harden beneath their fingers until it was prominent against the denim. They unbuttoned, slid their hand inside their pants, and felt their cock stiff and hard and ready. They tried not to think about what they were. They hated the thought of using lesbians for their own enjoyment when they had a dick now. Were they just as gross as a cis man who believed everything was for the male gaze?

They blinked and tried to focus on the screen, the moans. They leaned forward and clicked *Yes*. A few minutes later, there was a knock on the door.

It was the cute smoker from downstairs, and she nodded confidently at Red as she came in. "Oh, hey look who it is," she smiled. And she did have a beautiful smile. She must have been playing with someone else before because she'd changed out of the crimson corset into a leather jacket and slacks. She gave Red a once-over and they might have imagined it, but her eyes seemed to linger for a second longer on their open jeans and their cock pushing against the tight material.

"You must be Jax?" Red asked. Jax wasn't like how Red had imagined her; she was hotter, actually. A bit intimidatingly so. With broad shoulders, cute winged eyeliner and a fresh fade that really showed off the sharpness of her cheeks.

"That's me," she said, putting her toolbox on the table

and making her way over to Red. She immediately sat on their lap and straddled their hips, leaning in close. Red placed their hand on Jax's thighs and took a moment to breathe her in. She smelt of salt and slightly cinnamony. Her cheeks were warm and flushed and she seemed a little out of breath, or was her heart just racing? "You're damn handsome," she said, looking Red deep in their eyes. Red resisted the urge to blush and look away. They held her gaze and enjoyed the feeling of thick thighs pressing into their legs, an intimacy they were long out of touch with. Jax seemed strong and assured but she had a kindness about her and Red tried to lean into it.

"So, you already know a bit about me," Jax said. "I'm a heating engineer, I like tools," she grinned. "I know you do too." She paused as if waiting for Red to say something, but they had gone a bit quiet. "I liked your profile," she said gently. "And I think we're here for similar reasons. I've been a dyke my whole life, and then at some point recently I had a fantasy about cock and I know I want it, just not, like, *boy cock*, you know." She put her hand on Red's chest and they gulped. "I want queer cock, enby cock. And I know you didn't say much on your profile, but you got me hot. We can take it chill, don't worry babe, I've got you."

She slid her hand to the back of Red's neck and leaned in to kiss them. "That okay?" With Red's nod, she kissed them deeper, her lips biting into theirs, her tongue finding its way into their mouth. She slid her hand downwards, down their unbuttoned jeans, onto their dick which was still hard and hungry. But Red's whole body stiffened and Jax immediately pulled back. "I'm so sorry babe, are you okay?"

"Yeah, it's not you, I'm sorry, I just –" But Red couldn't finish their sentence.

"Shall we try –"

"Can we just stop?" Red asked, and then, "If that's okay?" They felt the familiar shame as it crept into their limbs and filled them up. The seemingly inescapable fullness of failure, even towards this stranger.

After Jax left, Red sobbed gently into their shirt sleeve.

* * *

"Darling, you're tender as fuck and can also both top and sub like a damn king. Anyone would be lucky to have you."

The next week, Red was having dinner with their ex, Gin, who was in town for the week. Gin was loud and unapologetic about everything – from their granny cardigans to their politics. They were the kind of campaigner artist type that made all the gays swoon, and were currently touring the country with their second album. Although they were a couple of years younger than Red, they seemed older, and their pep talks were to match. They'd been doing their concerned auntie face as Red stuttered over the latest intimacy stuff they'd been struggling with.

"Who else have you told?"

"My therapist."

"Red, your fucking therapist!"

"They're good!"

"Love, you think I don't know that. Half the transes this side of the river are seeing them. But you need to talk about this shit. Not just in therapy, but in a way that exposes you a bit. In a way that's vulnerable and difficult for you. With people who've been through similar stuff. And then with people you fancy." Gin could see how uncomfortable that made Red, but they were a believer in uncomfortable truths.

Gin softened. "You can keep in your head about it, but it's not going to make it better, my love. You remember when I got my tits and I started dating that cis boy from that damn hipster area and on our fourth date he asked me if he could call me his daddy and I went home in fucking tears? Remember what you said?" Red was quiet, but they nodded. "You said you would show him who daddy was and the next week you spray painted *'daddy's disappointed in you'* on the front of his car."

Gin searched Red's face. Red was worn down these past few years; different. They had fought hard most of their life to change the world that everyone inhabited. And now that it was changed, they were weary and seemed distant. Gin felt Red had clung too hard to their will for change; let it become who they were rather than what they believed in. And now they were too shattered, too diluted with pain, to really let the joy and hope in. They couldn't see themselves unless they were situating themselves in a battle.

Gin leaned forward and took Red's hand. It was rough and warm.

"You're worth the fight," they said.

✳ ✳ ✳

"Password?" asked the doorbot.

"473113."

The bot handed Red a robe and towel as they entered.

"You've been before?" it asked.

"Yeah," Red replied.

"Would you care to fill out a quick feedback form about your experience at the centre? Your feedback helps us improve our services for your future enjoyment."

"Not today."

The corridor swirled and skipped around Red as they made their way to the elevator. Sighs and groans leapt from the rooms around them, and made the pictures seem strange, almost as if the images themselves were crying out.

Red had asked Jax if she would be up for meeting again, had explained their nerves a little bit – around the surgery and not having fucked anyone since, and how what they wanted badly was also something that terrified them so immensely. Jax had been sweet and supportive and offered to follow Red's lead. So, here they were.

Red took the lift to the third floor and checked out a couple of the spare rooms before choosing one with a massive bed and a beautiful potted wisteria against the back wall. They got cosy on the sofa and connected their tablet to the wi-fi, so they could use that instead of the centre's old computer. They answered the questionnaire, ordered a couple of beers to be delivered to their room, and found some porn which started with two butches in vest tops chopping wood together.

"Hey, my axe is feeling a bit rusty, do you mind helping me sharpen it?"

"Here, let me just give your shoulders a rub between all that hard work."

"Babe, you're all sweaty, can I take your shirt off?"

"Let me feed you a beer to help with that thirst."

Red slipped their hand down their jeans…

* * *

Red was out front in the smoking area, making a rollie, and thinking about Flip again when a handsome person with cropped hair sat on the step beside them.

"You look like you're lost daydreaming," they said, in a deep but soft voice. Their curls fell over their forehead and their lips were thick and dark pink. Red took a puff, feigned confidence. Jax had been so beautifully present with them, so attentive, so excited about their mutual pleasure. So why had Red still felt weird? They had felt the tingles of pleasure, watched themselves harden, seen Jax take their cock and enjoy it, but they still felt like an observer, not really present with any of it.

They took another puff of their cigarette. Their fingers smelt like sex. The stranger was looking at them curiously and Red couldn't help but notice the broadness of their shoulders and the veins rippling down their arms. This person was hot, ridiculously so, in a way that made Red a bit shy and self-conscious.

"I'm Adrian," the person said, holding out a hand. Red looked down at their raised veins and their short fingernails. "Is it your first time here too?" They kept talking before Red could answer. "It's fucking weird isn't it. No matter how much these places try to simulate it, they can't simulate this." They looked directly into Red's eyes, and their silver pupils flickered.

Red gulped but held eye contact.

"You like what you see?" they asked.

Silence. The rise and fall of Adrian's chest.

"Do you fancy a drink sometime?"

*** * ***

It was a Thursday evening and Red knocked nervously on the forest green door. Adrian pulled it open, leant in for a hug, and Red tried not to be weird about noticing the way they smelt – like orange and rose.

"Welcome, welcome, can I get you something to drink?" The living room was burgundy, with gentle lights and a comfy sofa. As Adrian left for the kitchen, Red tried to look politely away from their thick ass and hench shoulders. God, they were strong. So strong. Red wondered if they were on T or not. They wondered which Instagram transmasc they followed for their workout advice, and how silly it would feel to ask.

Adrian came back in to sit beside them, close. "How are you doing temperature-wise?" they asked. "I can turn the heating up if you like."

"I think you're really fit," Red said. Their heart was smashing against their ribs. "And I want to kiss you."

Adrian's lips were soft and sweet like tangerine. Red kissed them slowly at first, then deeper, feeling Adrian's hands run down their sides and their want thicken. They slid their tongue into Adrian's open mouth and bit playfully at their bottom lip. Adrian moaned gently in response, their shoulders dropping and their posture softening. Their jaw loosened as Red kissed along it, and their body sunk into the couch, their legs falling further apart.

Red worked their way to Adrian's neck, checked in with them, kept teasing them. They could feel Adrian's heart pounding against their skin. They bit tenderly into their flesh, took Adrian's chin and tilted their head back, enjoying their moans getting louder and less controlled. The buzz of traffic outside dimmed and Red's mind slowed.

They reached for Adrian's shirt buttons and made quick work of them. Adrian's belly was soft and beautiful and they wore a binder.

"You can take it off," they said. Red pulled the binder over Adrian's head. They giggled together at how that wasn't always the smoothest motion. Adrian pushed Red's head to their chest and Red ran their tongue over their hard nipples. Adrian's sweat was sweet and sticky. Red reached down to lay a hand on Adrian's jeans and discovered that their cock was protruding, hard, wanting. Adrian let out a deep sigh. "Can you take care of it?" they asked, and the question made Red's cock stiffen in response. They felt it this time, the want buzzing through their whole body, and they got down on their knees and unbuttoned Adrian's jeans to take out their throbbing cock and place it between their lips.

Adrian moaned until they came straight into Red's mouth.

"Swallow it," they said, and Red obeyed, their own cock so alert they didn't know what to do with themself.

Adrian reached down and slipped off their spent cock, all the while keeping eye contact with Red. "Fill me up?" they said, and it wasn't so much a question, but a plea. They stripped Red of their clothes and guided Red's cock between their legs.

It was incredible watching Adrian's face as they entered them. Red's mouth gaped and their eyes rolled back in pleasure. Adrian gasped at each thrust and Red was gentle with them because they knew their cock was big and they wanted Adrian to feel pleasure in every slight movement. Adrian pulled them close, kissed their forehead, and begged for more until Red was pinning their arms down and pushing deep, deep inside. God, Adrian's arms were good. They were thick and laced with muscle, and they twitched under Red's grip. Red watched Adrian's lips part, their nipples bounce, their body grind and shudder. And without even expecting it, Red was coming, oh so hard, inside of them.

Red rolled onto the sofa, breathless and confused but joyful.

"You needed that, didn't you?" Adrian said, and right then their confidence was so delicious that Red wanted to sink into them. They held out one of those ridiculously hench arms, and Red fell onto their chest. "Good boy," they said, as if they hadn't already given Red pleasure enough, and Red felt their cock stir again.

"It takes a while to get used to," Adrian said. "Mine did, anyway." Their heart was humming against Red's cheek. "The more I got used to it, the less I needed it. It's funny, that."

"Can we do this again sometime soon?" Red asked, their chest full like a piggy bank.

Masturbation Saved My Life

BY ANNA SANSOM

Content: *self-pleasure and empowerment, burnout, surrogate partner therapy, body autonomy*

I don't know which of us was more mortified: my 12-year-old best friend, or me.

I'd just innocently asked, while we were walking home from school, "What does masturbation mean?"

Her cheeks glowed red and she stared at the scuffed toes of her black, lace-up shoes. Despite her obvious embarrassment, being a true friend, she managed to stammer out an answer: "It's when you touch yourself. You know, because it feels good."

I didn't know. I hadn't discovered the joys of touching myself yet. Well, unless you count that time when I was around ten and wrapped a length of yarn around my waist, before threading it between my legs, and pulling tightly on both ends until I felt... What? Pleasure? Not a word or feeling I knew back then. Rather it was a fleeting feeling of yumminess. A bit like the first spoonful of chocolate ice cream at the end of a meal.

Back home, having said goodbye to my friend until the next morning, I did what I should have done before putting her on the spot: I opened up the dictionary.

There, in the pages of the Chambers 20th Century Dictionary, sandwiched between *mastoid* and *masty*, I read:

> **masturbation** *n.* stimulation, usually by oneself, of the sexual organs by manipulation, etc., so as to produce orgasm.

More words I didn't understand. I flicked over the pages:

> **orgasm** *n.* immoderate excitement: culmination of sexual excitement: turgescence of any organ.

This was feeling like a school lesson now. I closed the book and went outside to play.

* * *

As an older teen and in my early adulthood, masturbation continued to be a lesson I had to persevere with. I knew the bit about stimulating my genitals but I didn't have a clue about how to translate friction into something that felt pleasurable. I would rub and rub until I was sore, my vulva dry and weary, my clit limp and complaining. I still hadn't found that elusive 'feel good' factor.

Fast forward to my late 30s and I was propped up on some cushions with my legs spread wide. A woman sat between my thighs, her back leaning on my chest. We'd only met an hour ago but she was naked and my hand was gently placed on top of hers. Her fingers made tentative circles on her clit.

I was a member of a sex therapy team, working as a

sexual surrogate partner to support people of all genders in learning about their bodies, sex, and intimacy. The student had become the teacher. I'd come a long way – but I knew I'd still got a long way to go.

At that point, masturbation had shifted from something purely mechanical (and unfulfilling) to involving fantasy and my imagination (and a lot more orgasms). Through trial and error, on my own and with other people, I'd learned the type of touches that got me off. More importantly, I'd also discovered the circumstances I needed to feel arousal and just how vital it was to actively desire what could follow. Masturbation was a double act: my mind *and* body both had to be present for it to work. Sure, there were some occasions when I just needed the quick and easy release of a vibrator held firmly against my clit but, increasingly, I found myself needing something that had more meaning. A third member was about to join the party: masturbation was soon to become a spiritual practice.

The first time it happened, I was genuinely shocked. Instead of my usual fantasies of a lover touching me passionately and roughly until I was a trembling, moaning mess in their arms, this time I was alone. I pictured my cunt as a cauldron of fire. As I stirred the pot, sparks began to fly. I felt potent. Powerful. I spoke one word aloud as my hands danced over my vulva: *Mine.* My fingers entered me and the cauldron began to overflow. I was molten. My fire spread all around me. Now I was Phoenix and I was rising, rising, rising. *Mine.* My flaming feathers took me higher and higher and I was free of gravity. I soared up into the stars. Now I was a meteor. A ball of fire. Moving faster than the speed of light. I was the light. I was... *Mine.*

The orgasm that followed felt like an implosion. All the power I'd just connected with was drawn deep into my body – I contained an entire universe; a billion stars; infinite possibilities.

***

Life continued in the way that life does. Several years passed. I did my job (now as a health researcher at a university). I cooked my meals. I nurtured my relationships. But somewhere along the line, stress began to mount. I could feel it in the tension in my jaw. I started to grind my teeth in my sleep and my dentist advised me to wear a bite guard at night. My shoulders got painfully tight. I frequently had headaches. My libido suffered – I wasn't interested in sex or masturbation.

Eventually, I had to admit this was feeling like burnout. My inner flame was extinguished. I could no longer access my spark.

Oh.

Now what?

I'd spent two years training and working in the intimate setting of the sex therapy clinic. It offered a very particular type of therapy: surrogate partner therapy. The uniqueness of this work is that it involves three people: the client, the therapist, and the surrogate partner. The surrogate partner is there to help the client have *embodied* experiences alongside the talk therapy sessions with the therapist. There are clear boundaries around the relationships but, as the name suggests, sex *can* take place between the client and surrogate.

Of course, the definition of 'sex' is incredibly broad, and the surrogate's role could include all kinds of sensual and sexual activities – along with emotional connections (for what is intimacy without connection?).

Part of my journey with this work was learning to

become embodied, and learning to become connected to my intuition. I learned how to use my breath to centre and ground me. I learned how to listen to my body and how it felt when I got a clear 'yes' as well as a definite 'no' (and I learned how to respond when my body offered me a 'maybe'). I learned how to stay present to myself as well as to the other person. The three-hour-long sessions often felt like they flew by. It was mindfulness in practice. I experienced a state of 'flow'.

That's not to say that it was always perfect or that it didn't take a toll on me. That amount of presence and attention could leave me feeling too sensitised to the world and – at times, after a particularly intense or challenging session – I had to retreat into old numbing patterns of overeating and zoning out in front of the TV.

✳ ✳ ✳

Back to the burnout.

I'm using that term because it truly felt like the fire in my hearth had turned to ash. As I raked through the remains, however, I found one, small, glowing ember. I offered it a little of my breath and it glowed brighter for a moment. I knew I had to save this part of me. I had to nurture my ember back into roaring flames. But, to do that, I'd have to go gently.

I returned to my masturbation meditation; my *medibation*.

At first, all I could do was just breathe with one hand on my belly and the other resting over my heart. I moved my hand lower – now connecting my pelvis with my heart. And then focused my attention on my pelvis and the area between my eyebrows – my 'third eye' area in energetic/ woo terms. No expectation. No demands. Just giving *presence* and *connection* to my Self again.

I realised I'd become critical of myself and my perceived 'lack' of sexual energy. My body had stopped being a site of pleasure. Everything felt heavy and murky.

My ember flickered.

The next medibation was a one-word affirmation. Naked, I touched each part of my body lightly. I started from the crown of my head, then moved to my brow, my nose, my lips, my ears, my chin... Each touch was accompanied by the word 'love' spoken out loud. Then to my throat, my collarbones, my shoulders, arms and hands... My breasts, my ribs, my belly, my mound... My hips, my thighs, my knees, my feet... *Love*. I moved back up to cup my vulva with my palm. Did I want more touch there? I listened and waited for my body and my emotions to respond. *Yes*.

Gently, gently. Breathing more oxygen onto the ember. Allowing my breath to keep me present: *I am here*.

As my fingers explored this almost-forgotten landscape, little sparks of pleasure glowed like fireflies in the wake of my touches. I was bringing my sexual self back to life – even more than that – I was bringing life back to myself.

I appreciate this may sound overly dramatic but this wasn't just a one-time epiphany. The thing about being a human being living through these times is that stress is only ever a heartbeat away. We are surrounded by stressors that can accumulate and create all kinds of dis-ease in our bodies. I haven't yet found anything that can shield me from this so I've become reliant on having ways to counteract it. I picture it like rewinding an old VHS tape – I can go back to the beginning and record a new story over the top of what's gone before but I'm never starting with a brand-new tape. Eventually, I suppose, the tape will get tangled or snap, or the video player will stop working. That's inevitable. The circle of life and death. But, in the meantime, I get to start over.

Masturbation is one of the things I do to recalibrate. Spending time in nature is another. I need to have these *embodied* encounters where I feel my feet on the earth or in the sea, or the touch of my fingers on my breasts and cunt. I need to hear the sounds of birdsong or a river gushing, or my breath quickening as I am about to come. I need to smell and taste salty air or a forest floor, or the hot scent of my own desire. Without this embodied time, I am simply thoughts and habits, unconnected to anything that truly matters or brings me joy.

In my medibation/masturbation I have fucked the Universe. I have reclaimed lost parts of me. And I have discovered new parts. Most of all, I have made my sexuality mine. My energy. My choices. There's a tremendous amount of power in feeling this way. Life-giving power.

❋ ❋ ❋

After writing the first draft of this essay, I needed to feel this sexual potency again. I needed to know that what I was saying was true. I needed to prove to myself (and perhaps to you, dear reader) that masturbation can be that powerful. So, I gifted myself my time and attention, a bundle of accessories, and my breath.

Sunshine streamed in through the window and warmed my naked skin – allowing me to feel nature's presence as well as my own. My first orgasm was a deep internal one, an energetic inhale that filled me up and focused my energy into a glowing orange ball right in the centre of my pelvis. My second was the release, the exhale, sending the glow to every cell of my being and out beyond me into the world, like the radiating heat from a campfire or, perhaps, an eternal flame.

eternal flame (noun): a small fire that is kept burning as a symbol to show that something will never end Merriam-Webster Dictionary (accessed online 29 March 2024)

* * *

Betty Dodson (author of *Sex for One: The Joy of Self-loving*, masturbation teacher, sex educator and artist) wrote, "Masturbation is the ongoing love affair that each of us has with ourselves throughout our lifetime... [it] will get you through childhood, puberty, romance, marriage and divorce, and it will see you through old age." Betty lived to be 91 years old.

About the Editor

Anna Sansom (she/her) has written about 'imperfect intimacy' and 'expansive erotica' for over two decades.

Her previous roles include sexual surrogate partner at a sexual therapy centre in the UK, and Sex/Life Editor for DIVA Magazine (the leading magazine for LGBTQIA+ women and non-binary people).

Her writing has been featured in numerous anthologies and online, and she was runner-up in the Good Sex (writing) Awards. Her more-than-a-memoir, *Desire Lines*, was published by The Unbound Press in 2019.

Anna currently chronicles her *"living experiment of desire in queer midlife"* on Substack (annasansom.substack.com), and shares new erotica on TheoReads.com. She leads writing workshops and mentors writers who "write at the edges", specialising in topics other editors and writing coaches might find confronting or taboo.

* * *

Find out more and connect with Anna at:
AnnaSansom.com

Instagram: @Anna_Sansom_Writer
Facebook: @AnnaSansomWriter

Anna Sansom Publications

BOOKS:
Coming Close, 2nd Edition. Self-published, 2023
Wake Up Your Dragon. Self-published, 2023
Desire Lines. The Unbound Press, 2019
Coming Close, 1st Edition. Xcite Books, 2012

SHORT STORIES:
Steadfast and True in Take it Outside; Incision Press, 2025
Butterfly Heart in Best Women's Erotica of the Year, Volume 10; Cleis Press, 2024
Away with the Fairies in Skeins; Linen Press, 2024
The End in The Big Book of Quickies; Cleis Press, 2024
Anemone and Me in I Write the Body; Kith Books, 2023
Strictly Au Naturale in Girls Getting Off; Xcite Books, 2012
The Wedding Singer in Lipstick Lovers; Xcite Books, 2012
Party Girl in Tops and Bottoms; Xcite Books, 2012
Burnt Sugar in Delicious Divas; Xcite Books, 2012
Shortbread on the Beach in Tales of Travelrotica for Lesbians; Alyson Books, 2007

MAGAZINE:
Over 50 articles in DIVA Magazine (2013-2015)

ONLINE:
Short stories and personal essays featured on:
Autostraddle.com
Medium.com
OpenSecretsMag.substack.com
ReadAurore.com
Sugarbutch.net
TheoReads.com

Authors

AC ASQUITH (she/her) is a psychiatrist with a particular interest in the effect of mental health on our sexual lives and vice versa. She lived as a practising Muslim for most of her adult life and is now exploring a new life with her non-binary partner.

MERRYN AUGUST (they/them) is a queer fifty-something who likes to explore edges and taboos – in their writing and in their real life. They sometimes wonder if their fantasies stray too far beyond the edge, and share some of their darkest desires at **merrynwrites.com**

MEG-JOHN (MJ) BARKER (they/them) is a writer, zine-maker, collaborator, contemplative practitioner, creative mentor, and friend. They are the author of a number of popular books on sex, gender, and relationships, including graphic guides to *Queer, Gender,* and *Sexuality; How To Understand Your Gender, Sexuality,* and *Relationships; Life Isn't Binary, Enjoy Sex (How, When, and IF You Want To), Rewriting the Rules,* and *Hell Yeah Self Care.* They also publish zines, comics, and free books on the themes of plurality, trauma, consent, and creativity via their website **rewriting-the-rules.com**

JENNIFER COCKCROFT (she/her) is a multi-passionate creative whose writing blurs the boundaries between fact and fiction, playing with our inability to distinguish imagination from reality, and harnessing this magical superpower to its full potential. Holding a BA in Film & Television Studies and an MA in Linguistics (with a particular focus on literary stylistics), Jennifer also has a lifelong curiosity about what makes people tick. She combines this holistic view of the power of storytelling with more recent training as a coach and women's circle facilitator – holding supportive and expansive spaces that allow the full spectrum of human emotion and experience to be expressed and celebrated. A hopeless romantic at heart who indulges in the not-at-all-guilty pleasure of reading sexy books (ranging from sweet to seriously spicy), she dreams of meeting her perfect book boyfriend in real life. She also brings personal, lived experiences of chronic pain and invisible illness to her writing. Jennifer is currently working on her first novel and has many more stories waiting in the wings! With previously published pieces on creativity in Knitting magazine, she now writes regularly on Substack (**jennifercockcroft.substack.com**) and maintains a rainbow colour-filled Instagram presence (**@jennifercockcroft.author**).

KIMAYA CROLLA-YOUNGER (she/her) has spent more than 20 years as an integrative depth psychotherapist, with an ability to transmit a Field of Being that inspires permission resulting in brave, expansive discoveries. After a decade of offering her work through a Dakini archetype, her own particular flavour of Transformational Eros imbues all her offerings, engaging the Soul to move towards itself in a process of remembering. One of the founding members of The Association of Somatic and Integrative Sexologists, she studies 'true connection' as a sensuous capacity to feeling the body of life, and has a vivid understanding of this through a bodily, spiritual and perceptual lens. As a writer, she believes that reading can be a transformative act when the writing is connective, linking, embodied, and when nothing of the human spirit is excluded. She has led workshops in conscious sexuality at festivals and retreats in the UK and internationally, turning people on to Transpersonal Sexuality through the subtle body and creative imagination... a frontier deep within that longs to be known in each of us. You can find her online at **beingkimaya.com**

MARIA CYNDI (she/her) became a sexual health campaigner and advocate for the sexual rights of disabled people after watching a documentary about the female experience of sexual pleasure. In the programme, women from different ethnic backgrounds, social classes, relationship status, sexual orientation and age were interviewed about their sexual experiences. However, nobody from the disabled community was invited to contribute. The omission of disabled women in this programme prompted her to take action to highlight the importance of including disabled people in the conversation about sex and pleasure. She has been in an interabled relationship for twenty-nine years and has raised two children to adulthood with her husband. Throughout the course of her life, she has had to surrender her body to medical and community care professionals numerous times. Following sexual abuse in childhood, she rebuilt her life from the ground up and believes that everyone has the right to enjoy sexual pleasure regardless of ability, gender, race, class, culture, orientation or age. Reclaiming her body in adulthood and learning how to embrace her own pleasure, has been the most powerful and liberating experience of her life. This dynamic transformation has inspired her to do whatever she can to support disabled people in their pursuit of pleasure and sexual freedom.

BRITT FOSTER (she/they) writes visceral poetry and prose as well as speculative fiction that blends elements of fantasy, sci-fi, romance, and horror. She loves to explore the wholeness of the human experience by delving into the shadow. She also loves to write about queerness and sapphics. When not existing in an alternate dimension through her creative outlets, Britt enjoys watching songbirds eat from the bird feeder and sipping peach tea with oat milk. She can be found on Facebook and Instagram, both **@brittfosterauthor**

LILY JENKINS (she/her) is a married cis woman who is rediscovering her wants, desires and her Self at midlife. She is a multi-passionate creative who loves being in nature and by the sea. She enjoys reading and other forms of creativity and uses her writing as a way of exploring her sexuality and expressing her inner desires as an older woman. Lily lives on the UK south coast with her husband and her cat. You can find more of her writing online at **lilyjenkins. substack.com**

KAAN K (they/them, previously Yas Necati) is a writer and performance poet based in mid-Wales. They explore themes of queer and trans identity, diaspora identity, mental health, recovery, community and resistance in their writing. They have two poetry collections: *If I were Erol* (FourteenPoems, June 2024) and an as-yet untitled full poetry collection, also to be published in 2024. You can find them at **kaank.co.uk** and **@dream.with.kaan** on social media.

TRINE LEHMANN HANSEN (she/her) is a fairly cis-gender, so far more or less straight, 45-year-old single mom, who has been juggling stress, depression, and being a highly sensitive person (HSP). She recently jumped into the deep end of sex and dating to start exploring what she missed during her 12-year-long dry spell, and her some-what jumbled sex life before that. Trine admits to being a bit of an exhibitionist when it comes to thoughts and emotions, so she has been sharing experiences and insights from her journey in blogs and on her Facebook profile. She believes in the power of sharing raw, open, honest, non-expert stories because being touched and moved by someone else's journey is sometimes all it takes to ignite healing and transformation within ourselves. Aside from that, Trine has been passionate about personal development for decades and has worn the caps of podcaster, coach, and author. She is currently in the middle of writing a book with the working title: *How Joining a Sex-Dating Site Turned Out to be Cheaper Than Therapy – and a Lot More Fun!*

ESTHER LEMMENS (she/they) is a Queer Mystic, intuitive designer, and LGBTQIA+ advocate. She is an artist, writer, and gentle activist. Generally non-conforming, she likes to refer to herself as a 'rebel with a cause.' Their motto is *"do YOUR thing, YOUR way,"* and they passionately believe that authentic, unapologetic and at times radical self-expression is the most important gift we can give to ourselves – and to the world. Esther is a queer pansexual woman and the founder and host of the *Fifty Shades of Gender podcast.* She has just released her first course/workshop, *How To Be A Better Gender-Diverse Ally.* Esther moved to the UK from their native Netherlands in 1999, is a lover of food and tea, and has a weak spot for beautiful books and oracle decks. Fully embracing her neurodivergent witchy self, she hugs trees, talks to cats, and doesn't care if people think she's weird. Find her at **estherlemmens.com** and **fiftyshadesofgender.com**

ALYX MARSH (they/them) is a 50+ late-in-life, non-binary bi/omni person using writing as a creative outlet to discover who they really are. Happy to age but not get old, Alyx is a born and bred Australian living in Sydney who loves tea and biscuits, being outdoors and adding to their tattoo count.

JOY MOATES (she/her) is a writer and artist living in a magic cottage near the beach in southeast Florida. She can usually be found with sand between her toes and dirt under her fingernails, gazing at the moon. A teacher of sensual movement and yoga, she has written and published two books, *Embracing Your Wild Feminine* and *Naked*. You can find her online at **joymoates.com** or Instagram (**@joymoates_writer**)

BEAR PHILLIPS (he/him) is a lover, a trauma-informed bodyworker, and an intimacy, dating & relationship coach. In his coaching, he works primarily with men around questions of masculinity, and how patriarchy impacts our ability to have meaningful and authentic relationships. Bear has been involved in various forms of therapy and personal development for more than half his life and recently completed his training in *Compassionate Inquiry* with Gabor Maté. His first book – *Feminism Will Make a Man Out of You!* – is due for release in 2025. Find him at **bearphillips.co.uk** and on Instagram (**@bear_phillips**) and Facebook (**Bear Phillips - The Feminist Love Coach**)

JULES PURNELL (they/he) is a multiracial, non-binary, transmasc, queer kinkster. They are an AASECT certified sexuality educator, collector of erotica and LGBTQIA+/kink ephemera, sometimes professor and sometimes professional slut. They have been published in a few anthologies, (*Trans Bodies, Trans Selves*) spoken on a handful of podcasts, (*Sex Ed in Color*, NPR's *Life Kit*) and featured as a guest speaker for a variety of events related to human sexuality. Jules hosts play parties, runs workshops, and daydreams about buying a church to reclaim the harms done by organized religion for slutty queers everywhere. They are passionate about the nexus of spirituality and sex as a site of healing and liberation in the face of carnophallogocentric capitalism. When not engaging in the slut life, they are a restorative justice practitioner and queer parent residing in Western Massachusetts. You can find them on Instagram (**@jmpurnell**)

EVE RAY (she/her) is a bisexual trans woman and dominant kinkster, based in the English Midlands. She has been blogging about all things to do with sex and sexuality, and writing smutty stories, for over a decade. Her work has been published in a number of printed anthologies as well as on the FrolicMe.com website. She is a passionate defender of both LGBT and sex workers' rights. Away from writing she is a keen runner with several half marathons under her belt. She also loves motorsports and claims to be a connoisseuse of malt whiskies. You can read more of her writing on her website (**evestemptations.wordpess.com**) and follow her on Twitter (X) **@EveRay1**

ANNA SANSOM (she/her) is queer in all regards and endlessly curious about how we experience and express our unique sexual selves. She started writing erotica over two decades ago and has had a full-length erotic novel published and several short stories in anthologies and online. She also used to write the Sex/Life pages for DIVA Magazine, and has trained and worked as a sexual surrogate partner. In 2019, her most intimate work to date was published. Part memoir, part erotica, and part poignant questions for the reader, *Desire Lines* invites us to ask the questions – and explore the answers – which lead to greater understanding and enjoyment of our sexual selves. Anna has a PhD in occupational therapy and is the co-creator of *Foundations of Pleasure,* a guided journey for women who want to reconnect with their pleasure, sensuality, and sexuality, using creative, playful, and empowering personal practices. She loves drinking tea, swimming in the sea, and talking to her cats. She shares her*"living experiment of desire in queer midlife"* on Substack (**annasansom.substack.com**). You'll also find her online at **annasansom.com**, Instagram (**@Anna_Sansom_Writer**) and Facebook (**@AnnaSansom Writer**).

ESTHER WILD (she/her) is the nom de plume of a writer who is deeply moved by sharing their lived experience of life as a legacy, and a catalyst for change. Esther writes from the deep shadows, and vulnerability. Her words are offered from wounds that are in the slow process of healing. Her writing, raw insights, and experiences are given with humanity, honesty, and joy.

Permissions Acknowledgements

Printed in Great Britain
by Amazon